Thomas Edward Brown

The Doctor

A Manx Poem

Thomas Edward Brown

The Doctor
A Manx Poem

ISBN/EAN: 9783744765947

Printed in Europe, USA, Canada, Australia, Japan

Cover: Foto ©Andreas Hilbeck / pixelio.de

More available books at **www.hansebooks.com**

THE DOCTOR

A Manx Poem

BY

T. E. BROWN, M.A.

Late Fellow of Oriel College
Author of " Betsy Lee," " Fo'c's'le Yarns," etc.

LONDON

SWAN SONNENSCHEIN & CO.

PATERNOSTER SQUARE

1891

THE DOCTOR.

STORIES ! stories ! nothin but stories !

Spinnin away to the height of your glories !

And if I must, I suppose I must,

And you suspectin, I wouldn' trust,[1]

And sittin there all the time, and thinkin—

Is it true he's tellin ? and nudgin and winkin.

Now, bless my soul ! what for would I go

To tell you lies ? You're foolish though !

And there's odds of lies, for the matter of that,

For there's lies that's skinny, and lies that's fat;

And lies in fustian, and lies in silk,

And lies like verjuice, and lies like milk ;

And lies that's free, and lies for sale,

---

[1] I rather think.

And rumpy lies, without a tail;
Grew in the garden and picked in the woods,
Bubbles blew with the divil's suds;
Lies that's sweet, and lies with a stink at [1] them;
Lies like the dew that'll go if you wink at them,
And some as hard you couldn' break them
With a sledge [2]—aw, my lad knows well how to make
    them!
Haven' he got the tools to his hand
Down there? And the fire! Aw, he works them
    grand!
For it isn' every fool that's fit
To make a rael good lie, that'll sit
On her keel, and answer her helm—no! no!
Just try it, Bob! Just try it though!
Well put together! you're took on the sudden?
You couldn'? Didn't I tell ye ye couldn'?
Lies! what lies! the things I'm tellin
Is the abslit [3] truth—ax Neddy Crellin!

     [1] Of.   [2] Hammer.   [3] Absolute.

Ears is ears, and eyes is eyes,
And fax is fax, and that's the lies !

The Docthor ! The Docthor ! well, well, well !
The Docthor ! poor ould Docthor Bell !
Aw, I liked that man—I did though, for sure ! [1]
Uncommon good he was to the poor !
And free and hearty, but never much
Of a quality Docthor, nor regardin for such ;
Nor buckin up,[2] the way he might,
But proud to the lek, and very quite ; [3]
And keepin back—aw, keepin back
Reglar, and allis very slack,
Such times that they'd be sendin the gig,
Or the horse, aw, he didn' care a fig,
But take his own time, and the coachman swearin
At the door, for an hour, and the Docthor hearin,
And takin no notice, but readin the paper,
And " Doctors is chape, but time is chaper."

[1] Really.   [2] Pushing.   [3] Quiet.

And rap-rap-rap, and ring-ring-ring !
And the Doctor as happy as a king !

And—" The missis is took very bad with them,
       sir !
And you're wanted most partikkiler ! "
And—" I got the gig," and " are you asleep ? "
" Aw, she'll keep," said the Docthor, " she'll keep !
       she'll keep ! "
Aw, middlin rough, I tell ye, eh ?
Rough and careless lek that way.
For he didn' want their company
Nor their money neither, aw, he'd let them see !
But if a poor man's wife was shoutin,
Or some ould granny's innards routin,
Or fever, or fits, or tight in the breathin,
Or a child screwed up agate o'[1] the teethin,
Or drowned, or run over—no matter what !
Out on the door, and off like a shot !

[1] On account of.

Rich he wasn', nor never could be.

Savin he wasn', nor never would be—

Aw, the hand in the pocket, and out with it all—

As natheral, as natheral !

But the all wasn' much—aw 'deed[1] it wasn',

Maybe only a key, or a lump of rosin,

Or a bit of string, and pokin and pokin,

And heisin,[2] and divin, and allis jokin ;

But gettin very red in the face,

And divil a screw. And the shamed he was !

And—"Never mind, Docthor ! aw, never mind !"

And—*Wasn' he kind, and wasn' he kind!*

And—*The will was as good as the deed, for all ;*[3]

But bless ye ! of coorse there wasn' no call,

Nor the one of us wanted a penny of him,

Faith ! it's a deuced sight rather we'd gav him.[4]

A Docthor ! aw, it's right no doubt—

Somethin just to be haulin out

---

[1] Indeed.

[2] Hoisting = lifting.

[3] After all.

[4] We would have given to him.

For the kids—a lozenger or the lek—
Of coorse! of coorse! one might expec'—
But money! We warn' that poor! Didn' Peter
Find it in the haddock? And hav'n' the crayther
Got the mark of the ould chap's thum
Where he squoze it? But as for a drop of rum,
Or whatever was goin—gin, or brandy,
Or jough,[1] or the lek, it come very handy
To the Docthor, I tell ye; aw, never say no!
"Thank you, kindly," and down you go!
Aw, he could do well with it, he could!
And 'deed I'm thinkin it run in the blood.
And nice it was to see him takin it,
Smilin that way, and suckin and slakin it
Sweet in his throat, and the very belly of him
Risin to meet it, and warming the jelly of him!
And—"My cumplimans!" and the twist of the
    hand!
Aw, the rael fine ould gentleman!

[1] Ale.

Now, a drunken docthor is rather danger's,

You'll be sayin, and aisy might seem to strangers;

But them that knew him knew the differ,[1]

For never no man was brewin it stiffer

Till[2] the Docthor, mind! But give him fair play!

Five glasses or so, and, by gough! I'll lay

It was only the steadier he got—

And the head that was at him—as round as a
    pot,

And as big as two—aye, big altogether,

A fine strong man for any weather.

Aw, the Docthor had room! for there's chaps that
    small

And pinched in the guts, they won't do at all,

Nor can't hould on. Chut![3] Botheration!

The Docthor had the accommodation!

And if so be he was sprung a bit,

He knew himself when he wasn' fit,

[1] Difference.   [2] Than.   [3] Tut.

And wouldn stir—aw, steady still !
And sensible ! allis sensible !
" I'll just look round in the mornin," he'd say,
And of coorse they had to go away.
But clever ! bless ye ! that's the man
That was the clever ! aw, a terrible hand !
With the bleedin and that, and, high or low,
What was there that he didn' know ?
Arbs and roots and putrifactions ![1]
Bills o' passils [2] and vulgar fractions !
Birds and beasts.   Like Solomon
In Kings it's tellin, ould David's son,
The wise he was, and put in the Bible,
For the wise he was, but unforntit li'ble
To women, and that's the way it is,
There is'n one of us hasn't a list
To port or starboard, either way—
"Some likes coffee, some likes tea !"

---

[1] Petrifactions.   [2] Bills of parcels (in arith.).

Well, he was clever though—let him alone!

Every jint and every bone,

And every stave in your body—chut!

I believe the man could have made a foot,

Or a hand every bit as good as new,

And put it on with a slick of glue

Or the lek, and bless me! ye wouldn' have
  knowed

(The natheral) it hadn' growed.

Didn' he take a man's inside out,

And claned it and turned it round about

And in like a shot, and livin still

As comfible as comfible!

Aye, aye, did he! And a fellow's head

That was broke at[1] a gauger and left for dead,

What did he do but trimmed it a bit,

And put another lid to it

As nate as you plaize, and says he to the gauger,

"You'll not break that in a hurry, I'll wager!"

[1] By.

I know the man, a chap with one eye,
And gove [1] to fightin—and divil the lie!

I don't know in my senses had he a charrim [2]
For everything, for the books that was arrim ! [3]
And the picthers—aw, you never saw !
Pieces o' pessons—all as raw
And red as the shambles—painted lek,
And some all over a sort of a speck,
Like these dirty flies agate o' [4] the beef,
And things in bottles that come to grief,
Bein meant to be born, but never wasn',
Soakin in spirits, and never a pazon
Done nothin for them, but spoilt in the moulds
Someway—bless their little sowls !
And hadn' he a skeleton hung
Behind the door ? And the way he flung,
His dry ould chopsticks round ye ! grippin,

[1] Given.   [2] Charm.
[3] At him = his.   [4] At work upon.

And grinnin ; and you goin duckin, and dippin !

And houldin on with a click of a spring

Made fast to the hinges, all bones and string

And wire, and a kind of a sort of a trigger,

And rittle-rattle, the boosely [1] ould nigger !

And knives and screws, and prokers and lances,

It was fit to frecken [2] you out of your senses :

It was, for sure.[3]   And a big white dummy

With cipherin on his head ; [4] and a mummy

Brought from Egypt at some French divils,

And catgut, and pinchers set on swivels—

And—— God knows what ! But it wasn' them !

No ! that wasn' the way it came

To the Doctor, but just the head he got,

And the heart, and knowin every dot

Of a man, and lovin them, and thinkin

What were they like, and their eatin and drinkin—

Proud, lek proud, and rejicin in them—

---

[1] Beastly.

[3] Really.

[2] Frighten.

[4] Phrenological head.

And if the divil *was* to win them,

Still there was the man, and the beautiful art

That was took to mortise every part,

And the power that was in, and the putty[1] jined,

And plaised and happy in his kind—

Man to man—aye, that's your size,

That's the thing that'll make you wise—

That's the plan that'll carry the day—

Lovin is understandin—eh?

Lovin is understandin. Well,

He'd a lovin ould heart, had Docthor Bell.

But careless—very careless, though—

Bless ye! and lettin hisself too low!

The clever he was, and the gentleman born—

It was a pity of him—and never car'n'[2]

To take his place, and the quality

Thinkin diamonds of him, and him on the spree

Weeks at a time, and clane forgettin

Who was he and what was he, and lettin

[1] Prettily.   [2] Caring.

The people talk, but simple as ever,
And humble and proud ; but aw, the clever !—
The clever !—the clever ! and Tom and Dick,
And all the lot, as thick as thick—
And likin him much, but very quite,[1]
And a kind of a feelin it wasn' right.
But glasses round, and very nice talk,
And Callow's wife agate of the chalk,
And the Docthor in the big arm-cheer—
Aw, much respected—never fear !

And " Misthress Callow ! draw your best !
And—listen ! fill the Docthor's glass ! "
No, I didn' like that—aw, 'deed ! I didn' !
And they shouldn' have done it ! no, they shouldn'.
But sippin as nice as a 'potamus—
And never no pride with the like of us !
Not him, I tell ye ! but quite contrary,
And callin Misthriss Callow " Mary "—

[1] Quiet.

And never talkin much, but sittin
And list'nin to others, and smookin and spittin,
And the chair a little back in the 'cess,[1]
And takin a terrible interes'.

That was the Docthor? yes, that was him
The very man! And, sink or swim—
Up or down, to laugh or to cry with,
That's the man I'd like to die with.

The Pazon? Yes! aw, yes! well, maybe—
Aw innocent! innocent as a baby,
And good and true; but, for all, a man
Is a man, and I don't know will you understan',
But you know there's people's goin that good
They haven't a smell for the steam of the blood
That's in a man; or, if they have,
They houlds their noses, and makes belave
They havn'. But the Pazon—no!

[1] Recess.

True and kind; and the ebb and the flow
Of all men's hearts went through and through him—
The sweet ould man, if you'd only knew him!
But the lek is in,[1] and meant is meant—
But the Docthor! aw, the different!

And it wasn' men only, but 'arbs and that—
I tould ye before—aw, he had them pat,
And all sorts of bases [2] and fowls of the air,
And fish of the sea, and everywhere
Where God put life it would give him a start,
And he'd take and catch it with his heart,
Trimblin mostly, and wonderin,
But bound to find out all that was in,
And never satisfied till he had it—
Isn' that the way with God that made it?
Only at ither[3] ends, you know,
Him above and us below—
Like men in a mine, that's got to be workin

---

[1] There are such people.   [2] Beasts.   [3] Either.

Two levels in one, and stoppin, and herkin,[1]
And the compass at them,[2] and keepin nix,
And list'nin for each other's picks.
And when they're together middlin cluss,[3]
They're workin like blazes who'll be fuss,[4]
And slishin, slashin, rock and spar
Till the hole is broke; and there they are!

"But it isn' that way with God at all,"
The Docthor would say, "for the thinner the wall
Between you and Him the slacker He is,
And not mindin lek; and if you persiss,"
Them was the Docthor's words, "He'll either
Go back, or go by; and it's foolish rather,"
He'd say, "you'll be lookin! And see a flower,"
He'd say, "partickler after a shower—
Wouldn' you think now (a rose or a lily)
He was goin to talk to you with it? But will He?
Not Him, bless ye! But back and back,

---

[1] Harking.   [2] Having a compass.   [3] Close.   [4] First.

And in and in, and laves no track—
Red and yaller! aye, just so!
And the more you know, the less you know!"
Funny talk! but lovin for all—
Everythin that was beautiful!
"A thing of beauty is a joy for ever,"
He was sayin. And the tender! aw, you never!
The tender he'd handle the like, and strookin
Their little leaves, and lookin, and lookin.
Beetles, too, and butterflies—
Aw, they'd bring a light to the ould man's eyes
That was good to look at; and then he'd 'splain
How they were livin. And after rain
It's out to the garden he'd be like a shot,
And down on the grubs uncommon hot;
And a lump of a case at him where he kep' 'em,
And[1] pinched the worm or the louse that could
    skep[2] him.

---

[1] Hardly.   [2] Escape.

But tangles! that was his delight!
Dredgin, I tell ye, from mornin till night!
And he'd have me out with him—just a little chap
That could work the paddles, and a sort of a trap
He'd rigged a-purpose—a scraper you'd call it,
To scrape the bottom, and heavy to haul it;
But keen! aw, keen! and a nettin to't
Rove with rings that would open and shut
Like a purse. And "Aisy! aisy!" he'd say.
And I'd be stoppin, and him haulin away,
And sweatin bad, and up he'd have it,
And over the side as right as a travit,[1]
And then the joy! the abslit [2] wild,
And shoutin just like a little child!
And "Look here! look here! look! look! little
    lad!"
Aw, you'd swore the man was going mad!
"Here they are!" and sortin them out
On the taff,[3] and twistin and turnin about

---

[1] Trivet.   [2] Absolutely.   [3] Thwart.

That I'd be takin notice, and puttin

The terrible names on them, and cuttin

The stones and the muck out of them, and squeezin

The little threads; and coaxin and teazin

The fringes, and spreadin them out on his sleeve,

But the delicate! you wouldn' believe;

And the soft and lovin, and a sort of a cooin

Goin at him [1] all he was doin.

And prayin, you'd think, and passin the stringers

Of the long sea grass betwix his fingers,

As if it wasn wrack [2] he had there,

But the holy bread, or a baby's hair.

And sometimes I'd be freckened [3] lek,

Or sittin wondrin on the beck, [4]

And the oars dropped from me, and my mouth as

  open—

A little chap! or may be hopin

There'd be oysters in, and sometimes laughin

[1] On his part.　[2] Seaweed.　[3] Frightened.　[4] Thwart.

The way he was actin, but not very often,
For he'd turn and he'd say—"That's very bad!
Don't laugh! don't laugh now! little lad!"
And you're laughin too? And it's long ago—
Laugh! laugh! But I liked the Doctor though!

Now, you'll be axin how could a man
Like him be losin himself that plan—[1]
Sittin there in a public-house,
And drinkin, and callin that dirty trouss [2]
By her name, and let his glass be fillin
At the lek of yandher,[3] and him quite willin
For them to pay? "Aw, dear!" says you?
"Aw, dear!" indeed, and very true!
"Aw, dear!" you says? "Aw dear!" says I—
"The shame!" says you, to which I rerply—
"The shame!" And "drinkin" was it, you said?
Aye, and took home, and put to bed
At "the lek of yandher!" or maybe alone

[1] Way.　　　[2] Slut.　　　[3] By such people.

Tryin, and trippin over a stone

On the shore, and lyin takin his doze,

Till the tide come floppin under his nose,

And the sniff of the water'd waken him up.

Bless me! hadn' the man a sup

One night in Douglas, and a book as big

As a Bible at him, and a thingummy-gig

Of a sort of a trough![1]   And how did they act,

But took and tied them on to his back,

And on to the horse? and whatever it was

Whether the water or whether the grass,

Or used of[2] a mill that was up that way,

The horse took straight for the inner bay,

And him that stupid he didn' obsarv her,

And over her head and into the harver.[3]

And " Murder ! " and flounderin about,

And the sentry hearin, and the guard turned out,

And fishin him up.   And " He'll take his death

---

[1] Probably an electric battery.   [2] Because he was accustomed to.
[3] Harbour.

Of could," they says. And in spite of his teeth
Off with his clothes, and rigs him straight [1]
In a little red jacket, and houldin a light.
And the fun them divils of souldiers had!
And—"Serjeant! give him the shillin!" they said.
And the Docthor quite content for all. [2]
And standin, smilin, against the wall,
And his poor ould face all drabbled in tears,
And—"My noble British Grenadiers!"
He says; says the Serjeant—"A strappin recruit!
And by jabers we'll give him a royal salute!"
And out with the fife and out with the drum,
And—"Steady! my lads! we'll see him home,"
And caught the mare, and "'Scuse me, your honour!
You're a tidy weight"; and heaves him upon her;
And rub-a-dub! rub-a-dub! never say die!
And the Docthor quite happy, and nice and dry!
And over the bridge, and away they go,
With a fol-di-rol-lol-di-rol-idy-o!

     [1] Immediately.   [2] Notwithstanding.

And away to the Lhen, and up to the door,

And a tántaran that was fit, for sure,

To waken the dead ; and the Misthress comin

With a light, and the Serjeant stoppin the drum-
min,

And—" We've brought you your husband, Missis
Bell ! "

And only her shift ; and—" Very well ! "

Says she as aisy as aisy, and out

With the candle straight,[1] and used, no doubt !

And—" I'll remember you in my prayers,"

Says the Docthor, sthrugglin upon the stairs,

And as dark as the divil ; and leavin the man,

Or lettin him off, you'll understand.

Aisy ! aye, aisy ! and used,[2] you know,

But a doeless sort of a woman though.

What for wouldn' she kick up a fuss,

The way that other women does,

Bein anyways respectable—

---

[1] Immediately.   [2] To such occasions.

What for wouldn' she give him his fill,

Ladlin it hot? And very right!

Comin home that way of a night!

But bless ye! No! Just "Very well!"

That's all you'd get from Misthress Bell!

No spirit! Chut! Not a bit! Nor standin

On her right, and givin it them from the landin.

Why, there's many a woman would have up with
　　the sash,

And soused the lot!—a set of trash

Like them to be gettin it in the papers,

And frecknin people with their capers!

No sailor wouldn' have done the lek—

Bless your soul! too much respec!

And more till[1] one can play at that game,

And very apt to be took the same.

But still you'll be axin how could it be?

And a man like that? Well, look here! d'ye see,

[1] Than.

I'll tell ye now, but wait a minute!

Fist us that bottle! Is there anything in it?

All right! The cow must have her grass.

Now, listen!—this is the way it was.

The Docthor wasn' Manx at all,

But an Englishman; and what ye may call

'Printiced, you know, to a docthor in London,

A dandy docthor, the way there abundin [1]

In a place like that. Aw, terrible grand,

Buckin up to the first of the land,

Drivin about in a carriage and pair—

You know the lek is at them [2] there.

And a footman, bless ye! And off he leps, [3]

And touches his hat, and rattles the steps,

And out comes the Docthor as nate as a pin,

And the cheerful—it's astonishin!

And the coat that's at him, shinin, by jing,

Like a pazon, or a raven's wing?

And *how is Masther, and how is Miss?*

[1] Abounding.   [2] They have that sort of thing.   [3] Leaps.

And slaps a guinea into his fiss,
Or maybe two, I wouldn' wonder,
But one at least; aw, divil the under!
And aisy earned; and out like a shot,
And on to the rest—a humbuggin lot!
But of coorse, the quality has their way,
And must have it, and let them pay.
And them big lazy lubbers with breeches
And stockins at them! Well, riches is riches!
And where the carcase is, it's sayin, thither
Shall the eagles be gathered together.
Aye, that's it! well—troubles and troubles!
That's where the Docthor got in hobbles.[1]
For there was a man they were callin " Sir John "
The Dandy Docthor was docthor upon.
Aw, that was the man with the money—aye!
And a house at him, maybe ten stories high—
And nothin but gool.[2] Chut! Nothin but gool,
Every chair and every stool!

      [1] Difficulties.   [2] Gold.

And the cups and saucers—high uncommon!

High, aw, high! And never no woman

For cook in the kitchen at them there,

But a sort of a divil they called *mounseer*—

French, it's lek, and cockin his chin,

And jabberin, and jabberin.

Aw, gool wasn nothin yandharwheres—

Hadn't they bank-notes in the chairs

For stuffin? And lookin-glasses 'd[1] show

Every bit from top to toe,

And beds that was workin on a swivel!

And pianoes! aye, scores! And as proud as the
    divil!

Now, the Dandy Docthor, you see, for all,[2]

Sometimes couldn' get round on the call

That was after him reggilar; and so,

Of coorse, the young Docthor had to go.

And just as good, and very much lekked,[3]

Special at[4] what they're callin the "*sec*"—

---

[1] That would.   [2] However.   [3] Liked.   [4] By.

Manin the ladies !—and a handsome man,

And no mistake. And six foot one,

If he was an inch, and handsome still

When he was an ould man; for there's some o'
    them will—

Aye, wore, of coorse, but you'll notice the signs,

And a ship may be wrecked, but showin her lines—

And a light in his eye, like a sweet strong juice

Of fire comin tricklin from a sluice

In his head, or his heart, or somewhere or another,

Strained, like enough, from the milk of his mother,

And kindly mixed: and very nice

To look upon, and the same in his vice—

And playin the flute most beautiful,

In the pocket at him[1] down at the Bull,

Three pieces lek, and screwed with a jint,

And puttin his ould lips to a pint,[2]

And tootlin away, and heisin[3] the lift

Of his eyes. And mayve the best of a shift

[1] His.   [2] Point.   [3] Raising.

Of miners sittin and listnin there,

And fit to cry, the sweet to hear

It was. And rough enough divils them,

But never rough, I tell ye, to him.

Aw, if the miners was there, by gough !

You darn' spit, and you darn' cough,

Nor breathin mostly, or you'd have a fist

Down your throat middlin slippy—and "hush ! "

　　and " whist ! "

And—"aisy there ! " and " silence ! " and "shoo ! "

You might ha' heard a pin—aw, it's true, it's true !

And him an ould man, and maybe half drunk,

And the head that shaky, and the cheek that sunk !

What 'd he be like, then, when he was young—

With his hair all curled, and his vice like the
　　bung

Of a barrel, and lookin every man

Straight in the face ? Aye ! what would he be
　　then ?

Aw, there's no mistake ! you may put it down !
The puttiest[1] man in London town !
What did ye say? *He couldn' have been !*
In London, too, where the King and the Queen
Is livin, and all the quality !
And the finest men would be sure to be—
Knights, and Lords, and Ladies high,
Colonels and Dukes. To which I rerply—
Who says they didn'? Of coorse they do !
But wasn' Docthor Bell livin there, too ?
Wasn' he ? wasn' he ? Answer me that !
Aye, you're lookin as cross as a cat,
Are you ? Well, you're ugly enough
Already ! My goodness ! he's takin the huff !
What is he sayin? Who will he lather !
He *wouldn' stand it from his father !*
Well, I wouldn' hev a temper like yandhar fool.
Bless my heart then, let him cool !
Deed on Bobby ![2] don't look towards him !

[1] Prettiest.   [2] Bobby indeed = Poor Bobby !

Huffed, is he, eh? And who regards him !

Now, listen to me! I'll bet you a crown

He was the puttiest man in London town!

Now, I'll stand to that, now! What's your talk?

How am I sure? Well, there's chaps that'll balk

The divil himself! Now, just look here !

It's aisy howin! Aw, dear! aw, dear !

How am I sure? To which I rerply—

I happen to know it! And "*Who am I?*"

Says you. To which—— But, of coorse ! of coorse !

A chap may be shoutin till he's hoorse,

And nothin but contradictin still ;

And it's very disagreeable !

Very—all along of that cur—

Now, I happen to know partikkiler !

Partikkiler ! do you understand ?

Partikkiler ! the puttiest man

In London. I happen—never mind the how !

Partikkiler—aye ! where are you now?

But avast this talk !

Now, you must know
There was no house the Docthor was useder[1] to go
Till[2] to this Sir John's. And, bless me! the diamonds
They were thinkin of him! and he "shutes my requi'mans[3]
To a T," says Sir John; and "Come, man! come!
Dear me! make yourself at home!"
Ailin often, or thinkin he was;
And maybe a little too fond of a glass.
So there the Docthor 'd be makin his call,
And liked uncommon at them all!
Aw, the Docthor was this ; and the Docthor was that!
And the very dog and the very cat
Was takin joy of him; and a bird
They had would sing the minute he heard

---

[1] More accustomed.   [2] Than.
[3] Suits my requirements.

His foot.   He had a way, I expec',

To hould communion with the lek.

And the sarvints! bless ye!   The man was free;

And the plannin and the schamin there 'd be

To get him down in the kitchen, though;

And kind to the high, and kind to the low;

And allis one of them bound to be poorly,

And " *Would he see her ?* " and " *Surely! surely!* "

And any excuse just to get a look

At his handsome face.   And even the cook

Would allow he was a good-lookin falla,

" Though   not   in   my   style! "   he 'd   say,   and   as
    yalla

As the yoke of an egg, and as ugly as sin,

And a bit of hair on the tip of his chin;

And he'd have a talk with the Docthor too,

And jabber away with his parley-voo—

And the Docthor givin him back as good

As he gave.   Aw, that's the man that could,

French or Hebrew, Greek or Latin,

All sorts of lingo, chittin and chattin
As quick, I tell ye, and *wee-wee-wee!*
And *Mossher Bell!* And fiddle-de-dee!
And the sarvints delighted, but wonderin still,
And sayin—" Isn' he terrible?"
But as for Sir John, from mornin to night
He'd never have had him out of his sight;
For the Docthor was that handy about him
The ould chap couldn' do without him.
Aw, the Docthor knew the very fit
Of all his notions. And there he'd sit
And tell him all the talk o' the town,
And who was up and who was down,
And the in and the out, till at last he wrote
To the dandy Docthor, and bound him to 't
That he'd allis be sending Dr. Bell,
For there was nobody suitin him as well;
And sacked the dandy. You see, at least
He was only gettin the name of the place—
Head Docthor to Sir John, you know,

And the money of coorse, but never to go !

And Dr. Bell, he didn objeck,

And paid the same, but special lek

Betwix him and Sir John.   Now, Sir John, it

    appears,

Was a widda man[1] in the teens of years,

And only one child, and his heart much set

Upon her, by the name of Harriet—

The only child that was at Sir John,[2]

And just about goin on twenty-one.

Aw, that's the gel that was the pretty !

The handsomest in London city !

Aw, you'll take that, will ye ?   Well ! well ! no

    matter !

But you'd batthar[3]—eh ! it's like you'd batthar !

Aye—and it's middlin funny though,

If a man's goin a callin[4] handsome, it's *no !*

And *him !* and *ger*[5] *out !*   But if contrary

---

[1] Widower.   [2] Sir John had.   [3] Better.   [4] Being called.   [5] Get.

It's a woman, aw, then you're agreeable, very!

And pricks up your ears; and *dear!* thinks you,

There's a gel in the case! and handsome too!

Aw, bless me! and perfectly willin of[1] it,

Well natur is natur. But drov[2] it! drov it!

Now, this young gel was clever though,

As well as handsome, and lettin them know,

And a bit of a scutcher,[3] and orderin,

And every place as nate as a pin,

And couldn' stand no huggermugger

· About, and sarvin the tea and the sugar;

And weighin the mutton, and weighin the beef,

And wouldn' have no dirty ould thief

Of a housekeeper—or whatever they call them—

Betwix her and the sarvints, but would overhaul
  them

Herself like the mischief; and a book, and settin

ʻ What was she givin and what was she gettin;

---

[1] Admitting.   [2] Drop.   [3] Notable body.

Aw, strict, I tell ye, but terrible good

And righteous lek. Aw, the grand ould blood

That was in her, makin every limb

So sweet and so true that she looked to swim

In a light of glory and loveliness,

All about her, and fillin the place

With the right sort of spirit wherever she'd be—

And a sweet-smellin savour of honesty !

And for all the [1] strict, they were lovin her

You wouldn' believe ! aw, deed they were.

Happy and holy and undefiled,

And twenty-one ! aw, bless the child !

And terrible dutiful to the father,

But quite ; [2] and freckend [3] of him rather.

And him as proud as proud could be

Of her ; but a rough ould chap, ye see,

And of coorse he'd seen a deal of life

And wickedness, and lost the wife,

A middle-aged man, and took his fill

[1] Notwithstanding she was so.   [2] Quiet.   [3] Afraid.

O' the lek, and chewin the cud of it still,

And swearin for he couldn' do more

Till [1] chewin the cud. Aw, hard at the core,

And full of the world and the things of the world;

And nothin in him for the child to curl

Her soul around. Aw, a divil! it's true:

And rather a dirty ould divil too.

And not much truck [2] between the pair,

But dutiful, dutiful, reggilar.

It was the Docthor that he was takin to,

For of coorse the Docthor was bound to know

About all the divilment that was in,[3]

And this and that, and a heap of sin,

And all the rigs, and the crops, and the weather,

And who. and who was goin together,

And all the bag o' lies ould Nick

Shakes out every mornin for his childer to pick.

But I tell ye the Docthor shouldn' ha' done it,

And hard to stop the once he begun it—

---

[1] Than.   [2] Intercommunication.   [3] There was.

Aw, very wrong and foolish it was,

And comin home to him at las'.

But the Docthor! the Docthor! the Docthor still

At Sir John.[1] And the 'tention and the skill,

A miracle! a miracle!

He was swearin—the way he'd fixed his gout—

And "Chut!" he'd say; "what are you talkin
   about?"

He says, "I've took him by the hand,"

He says, "and by gough I'll make him a man."

"Yes," he says, "he's safe," he says,

"He's all right, I tell ye; the very first place

In this counthry," he says, "is the place for him,"

And no mistake but he'd have that same!

And where he'd spake for him, and what would he
   do—

And the cusses flying like Waterloo—

And "a divilish willin chap; and a wag,"

And "game," he'd say. Aw, the terrible brag

---

[1] The subject of Sir John's conversation.

He was takin out[1] of the Docthor! "by gorrum!"
He says, "the King'll be sendin for him."
And "the useful! the useful! you couldn' tell!"
And nobody like Docthor Bell.

And that was true! It's useful he was,
For whether a dog, or whether a hoss,
Or a man, or a maid, or an ox, or an ass,
Or everythin that is his—mind you!
The Docthor could tell the very screw;
Aw, fix it to a dot—he could—
To a dot, I tell ye; and understood
All about lawin and every spree,
And leasin lek, and proppity.
Aw, useful! bless ye! there's no know'n!
And handy uncommon, whatever was goin—
Big parties and that; and tasty show[2]
With the flowers, and decoratin you know—
And managin, and who to ax,

---

[1] To take brag out of = To brag about, praise.   [2] Very.

And a hammer at him, and a paper of tacks,

And fixin. And all the servants delighted

And runnin. And pounds of candles lighted—

Bless ye! all the house in a blaze,

And the Docthor knowin all the ways;

And how should it be, and when to begin,

And *mind*, *now !* *mind !* and orderin,

And well acquent with all the stars,

Sthroullers lek, musicianers—

Punch and Judy divils—chaps

That's glad to come for the bits and the scraps!

And dangerous to get drunk though, very,

Gin or brandy, port or sherry—

All as one;[1] and hardly seein

The book afore them, and tweedledeein

Like mad, tell they cannot tweedle no more,

And goin a puttin[2] to the door,

And collared at[3] the police, never fear!

Aw, dozens of fiddles! aye, dozens there!

----

[1] All one to them.　　　[2] Being put.　　　[3] By.

Goin like the deuce, and rub-a-dub-dub—
Tramhurns[1] and things. Aw, just like a club!
Jinglin-janglin enough to have stunned ye,
Just like a club o' Easter Monday;
And the Pazon goin in the front, and struts out
Like a cock, and the band a blowin their guts
 out.

Now, Sir John was ould, but he was fond
Of company was ould Sir John—
Aye—and glad if a body would take
The trouble of shuperintendin the lek—
And nothin to do but to look as big
And as grand as he could; and a beautiful wig
Made fast that never no body could pint
Azackly[2] the place he had the jint.
And a noddin here, and a gruntin there,
And backin and gettin into a chair,
A' purpose for him. And cards, and a set

----

[1] Trombones.   [2] Exactly.

Of ould chaps like hisself; and they'd dale and
 they'd bet, ·

And they'd cuss—very comfibil—and keep

At the cards till the lot o' them went to sleep!

And Docthor Bell of coorse head man.

And so you'll aisy understan'

How it happened betwix them two—

The young missis, I mane, and the way they grew

Very thick, and much together.

And that's the way, you see, you'll sleddher[1]

Unknownced, and slip and slip again,

Till over you go, and it's love that's in![2]

Head over ears—the way they're sayin,

But gradjal! gradjal![3] for love will be playin

A terrible long game sometimes—

Aw, 'deed he will! and the divil climbs

Inch by inch, but he climbs, for all;[4]

---

[1] Slide unconsciously.   [2] That is there.
[3] Gradually.   [4] Notwithstanding.

And let your main royal be ever so tall,

It's him that'll stand upon the truck.

And—down with your colours! By gough! you're
took!

Down with your colours! down! I say—

Aw, you're a fair prize, anyway!

The little monkey with his bow and arris,

Lek he'd be afthar shootin sparris—

You've seen in the valentines, small but spunky!

Aw, the little monkey! the little monkey!

He'll do it, he will; aw, there's not much doubt

He'll do your bizness. Chut! get out!

Bless ye! how could they manage it

That it wouldn' be, and her to sit

At a little bit of a table there,

And him a standin behind her chair,

And her to be calkerlatin lek,

And him to prove it all correct!

And if she looked up now, what would she see

But a man that was made as a man should be?

And if he looked down, what was the sight?

A woman as beautiful as the light!

And her lookin up, and him lookin down,

Is the way it was mos'ly,[1] I'll be bound!

Nor it isn' natheral, I'll assure ye,

To be allis lookin straight before ye!

And aisy talkin—but, listen to me!

How would it be now? how would it be?

The lovely scent comin off her hair,

And the curly rings, and the neck all bare,

Excep' a little thread or so

Stragglin, lek not knowin where to go!

And, aw, the beautiful divide

Tha'd[2] be there—the white! and the purified!

And the tips of her ears. They're soft little things

Is them, like indiarubber springs—

Nice uncommon to feel. Hurroo!

I'm off my coorse! This'll never do!

[1] Mostly, generally.   [2] That would.

You're laughin, Bobby? Aw, he has me!
The stuff I'm talkin though, God bless me!
But still now mos'ly it's hard to tell—
But a boy is a boy and a gel is a gel;
And put together lek that way,
And their breaths goin mixin like the hay
Of a sultry everin,[1] and near
Enough to one another to hear
The come and the go, and the click o' the heart;
And now and then a little start,
And a catch on the cogs, and houldin in—
Aw, it'll cook your goose astonishin!

And bad enough in the town, but wuss
When ould Sir John gave a rattlin cuss,
And it's on to the country, at your sarvis!
The Docthor must come with him for harvis!
Such times the shootin would be goin,
And horses to ride, and boats either rowin

[1] Evening.

Or sailin, and fishin. Aw, ye never seen!

A mortal grand place it must have been.

Aw, that's what done it altogether

Betwix them two. And no talk o' the father,

Nor the how, nor the when, but married they'd be

Some time or other—ma chree![1] ma chree!

Aye, that's the very way it is—

A kind of a sort of drunkenness.

I'm told she was proud, too, all the same;

And they're hard to fall in love is them,

But fell[2]—chut! bless ye! there's nothin lek them!

No! for you'll neither bend nor brek[3] them!

For pride is hard and love is soff—[4]

But the two together—that's the stuff!

Harder till[5] hard! the way they're mixin

Two metals in one for the hard,[6] or fixin

The die, very slow in the soak,[7] mind you!

---

[1] My heart.   [2] Once they have fallen.   [3] Break.
[4] Soft.   [5] Than.   [6] Hardness.   [7] Soaking.

But takin the colour through and through!
Takin—aye! aw, long in the steepin—
Takin—aye! takin and keepin!
And didn' they ax the father? No!
Certainly not! A rum sort of go
To be axin him! What for? My conscience!
What for? Now really! What sort o' nonsense
Is that to be axin! Says you, *What for?*
Says I, because they didn' dar![1]
Dar, says you. Yes! *dar*, says I!
They should, says you. To which I rerply—
Certainly not! Now, then, go on!
Certainly not! Aw, I see you're done!
Very well, then—done it is—
Interruptin! Idikkiliss![2]
The reason they darn? Well, wait a spell
And you'll hear the reason. Waitin's well.
Aye, indeed! Now, the counthry air
Is terrible for love, I'll swear—

[1] Dare.　　　　[2] Ridiculous.

Terrible to make it grow,

And take a root, and blossom and blow

Like the roses, and all the flowers. The lek

Isn' in towns, and you can't expeck.

For people is lovin in towns of coorse,

But it isn' the deep, and it hav'n' the force,

Nor wholesome lek, and sweet, the way

It is in the counthry, with cows and hay,

And all to¹ that; but a sort of a bother,

And a aggravatin one another,

Or makin believe; and a hum and a huff,

And none o' the juice o' the rael stuff—

Somethin like the milk they've got,

Half of it water. And whether or not,

No light in the sky, no bird on the wing,

A sort of a dirty gasey thing!

Isn' the air all rotten? Yes!

And lovin the same—that's the way it is.

That's the way in the towns, you see;

¹ All the rest of it.

E

But the country—aw, dear o' me!

Well, back to the town, though; back to the town:
And it's lek enough it's there they foun'
The differ,[1] but takin it with them—eh?
Aw, come out o' that! What do you say?
Apt to be foolish? That's allowed!
But aisy! aisy! the both o' them proud,
Proud of each other, and very plaised
The love was at them;[2] that's what aised
Their hearts uncommon, thinkin—what?
Thinkin they were chised,[3] lek, from the lot—
Chised complete; and never no man
Nor woman, I tell ye, but the one—
Just the one; and then—— No matthar!
Give it up! the wuss, or the batthar—
Just the one! Aw, that's the style;
For love is straight[4] like a little child:
You loves me, and I loves you;

[1] Difference.   [2] They had the love.   [3] Chosen.   [4] Just.

So what are you wantin us to do?

Spake to the father? Go to pot!

Certainly not! certainly not!

No, no! Bless your soul! fair play!

Time enough for that, thinks they;

Or never didn' think nothin about it;

Never axed, and never doubtet—

Some way, some day. The world is wide,

And driftin, driftin with the tide.

And driftin is very pleasant, too,

When the sea is calm and the sky is blue,

And you've got the littlest taste of a breeze,

Just enough to make a baby sneeze;

And your head on your arms, and your feet on a

taff,[1]

And nothin drawin, fore or aft—

Chut! as happy as Nicodemus,

And knowin you're out of the track o' the

staemers;

---

[1] Thwart.

And maybe a bee comin bummin by,
As if he was in the notion to fly
Far, far away, where there's brighter flowers
And sweeter honey, he's thinkin, than ours—
Or a bit o' thistle-wool comin skippin
Head over heels; or oars a dippin
Out on the Trunk,[1] and all the nisin[2]
O' the land goin into one, surprisin—
Dogs and cows—lek a sort of confusick,[3]
Makin a wonderful mixthur o' musick;
And the very land itself'll go
Like an urgan[4] playin, soft and low!

Bless me! where am I now? A *calm !*
And *driftin !* 'Deed, I think I am.
But driftin, if it's driftin your for,
Two together—there you are—
That's the sort! No need to rest

---

[1] A famous fishing ground.   [2] Noise.
[3] Confusion.   [4] Organ.

Your head on your arms when a lovin breast

Is ready to take it. Rest it there !

And driff—driff—driff, then, God knows where !

Aye, but that's it, for the man would be clever

That'd go on driftin and driftin for ever.

No ! it must come to an end at last,

And it doesn matter the slow or the fast,

Settin in on a point, or takin you aff,[1]

Nor how's your sheets, or what's your draff [2]—

It's up like a shot ! and *pull man, pull !*

Backards is backards, says Bobby the Bull.

But it soon came out in London for all,

The very next winter—a terrible ball

They were hav'n, lek maybe thousands there,

And the jingin and shovin, just like a fair.

And the Docthor not very careful though,

But took the fancy, and off he must go

Lonesome lek, whatever he had,

---

[1] Off.   [2] Draught.

And lavin the quality at it like mad,
And into the 'sarvatory, a place
Built on to the house, in a sort of a cess [1]—
They're keepin feerins [2] there, and the lek of them.
And glass you know, and a sort of a frame—
Cucumbars ? Well, you're makin me laugh !
Cucumbars ! What are you thinking of?
No ! but a house as big as a shop,
And flowers goin twistin over the top
Inside and out; and no dung nor beddin,
The way with cucumbars; and spreddin
Roundy lek, and glass, I stated,
And most magnificent titervated.

So that's the place where the Docthor came in,
Just soulerjin [3] about, in saemin; [4]
And rather dark in there, I'm tould,
And nice and fresh, and a sort of a bowl,

---

[1] Recess.   [2] Ferns.   [3] Soldiering, lounging.
[4] Seemingly.

And a spoot[1] goin skutin the water up,

Only just a little sup,

But givin a very pleasant sound,

Skutin and drippin all around.

Aw, a fuss-rate place! But it's lek I needn'

Be tellin you what was the Docthor heedin—

Aye, aye! You're right. Of course she was—

And a lad is a lad, and a lass is a lass—

Swells? yes! yes! but the proud white neck

Stooped, and all of a trimble lek,

Stooped though, stooped! Aw, never fear!

Much the same, from what I hear—

And no mistake! the ould, ould story!

And "Honey-soap!"[2] says Queen Victory.

Now, this dandy docthor I was talkin about

Was jealous of Docthor Bell, no doubt—

Mortal![3] And no wondher, you'll say,

Bein put out of the berth that way;

And watchin, watchin, like a cat,

---

[1] Spout.   [2] *Honi soit*, etc.   [3] Desperately.

And eyein his chance—aw, mind you that!
And there that night, and took up a pogician,
As the bobby said, like a fellow fishin,
And calkerlatin, and dancin the fly,
And fish about, but rather shy—
Just like I heard a preacher tell
The divil is fishin in the dubs of hell—
Watchin! the dirty thing! And took
The advantage of them two! Worse luck!
And crep', and crep', and saw them together,
And the kisses goin, and envyin rather,
Aw, envyin, by gough! And away
To ould Sir John, which was hard at the play,
And *somethin partickler*, and *wasn' able*
Just there, and got him from the table,
Swearin, though; and faith! he tould him.
Aw, then, the job was how to hould him!
And jumps like a lion shot at the hunter,
And "*Who?*" and "*What!*" and he'd go and
    affront her—

Confront is it ? All as one [1]—

And " Make love to my daughter ! " says Sir John,

" Make love to my daughter ! " And like to bust,

And the mad he clane forgot to cuss.

And the people begun to stare. But the dandy

Took him away, though, very handy,

And into the 'sarvatory another road,

And coaxin him, for the love of God,

To keep quite.[2] And " Be carm,[3] Sir John, be

    carm ! "

And scrunchin the teeth, and just like barm—

Foamin ! And *her*, he was sayin, *her !*

And, then—" Look there, Sir John, look there ! "

Look there, indeed ! Aw, the close ! the close !

And the four lips makin the one red rose—

Somethin worth lookin at, I'll swear !

Aw, a beautiful pair ! a beautiful pair !

" Rascal ! scoundrel ! villain ! thief ! "

Aw, the rose was broke—aw, every leaf !

[1] All the same.   [2] Quiet.   [3] Calm.

"Come out of that!" he says, and the string
Of his tongue was unloosed, and then full swing
The cusses come rollin fair and free.
And, "Is this your gratitude to me!
And you! Miss Madam! you! you! you!"
He was chokin lek; but the poor girl flew
Like a freckened bird, and in on the door—
The little one, I tould you afore—
And the dandy he got behind it, the way
She wouldn' see him! Aw, as good as a play!
But she did, and she gave him a look for all[1]
That was fit to pin him against the wall.
And he bowed very low, the sliddherin snake—
A dirty divil, and no mistake!

And what did the Docthor do? What could he?
Answer him? Chut! It was well he kept studdy,[2]
Aw, very studdy, and takin his part,
But studdy, except he gave a start

---

[1] However.   [2] Steady.

At something that the ould man said

About the young lady. Aw, then the head

Went up, and the eye was brought to the level,

And bedad the ould man had to be civil

For a bit, and backed, you see—the freckened

He was—rather further till[1] he reckoned—

And over a tub, and tripped, and comin

Against a image of a woman

That was there, and shook, and threw on the
    ground,

And broke; and maybe a hundred pound!

And black in the face, and the cusses as hot

As brimstone boilin out of the throat—

And the company comin runnin in,

And all the row and all the din—

And gettin to know, and glasses cockin,

And "Oh!" says the ladies, "Oh! how shockin!"

And drawin a one side, as if they meant

The Docthor to go. So the Docthor went.

---

[1] Than.

Then says an ould chap—and he gave a cuss—
"A strappin young fellow! She might have done
　　wuss!"

And what to do? Aw, bless your soul!
How would *I* know? Only I'm tould
The same man fought the battle well,
Aw, it's the rael stuff was Docthor Bell.
And up to the house the very next mornin,
And day after day, and the sarvints warnin,
If they'd spake to him, and he *would* see Sir
　　John—
Yes! he would, and he *should* see Sir John!
And all very well if he *could* see Sir John!
But the most o' the ould sarvints was forced to go,
Takin his part, o' coorse, you know.
'Deed I believe the lot o' them had
To leave, excep' Mounseer, and a lad
That was at them [1] there they were callin James—

　　　　　[1] They had.

You're wonderin I remember the names?
Aye! lek enough! But James and me
Was well acquent. So let that be.

Day after day, day after day—
Aw, it was a pity of him, any way!
Pity enough! And never no chance
To get speech with Sir John—aw, divil the once!
And letters! letters! Lave him alone!
And her of coorse never gettin none!
And tould at last at[1] a big new flunkey
To *cut his stick*, and rizzed his monkey,
And ups with his fist and knocks him down,
And nabbed at[1] the bobbies, and took and bound
To keep the peace, the way the law says—
And this and that—and five shillin and cosses.[2]
That's what they're callin *justice*, by jing!
Justice! There isn' no such thing!
Not for the poor man! no there isn'!

----

[1] By.   [2] Costs.

Down with the dibs, or go to prison !

That's the *justice !*   Aw, the beauties !

A executin of their duties !

" Empty puss—nothin does !

Full bags—nice nags—

Money is honey—my little sonny !

And a rich man's joke is allis funny !"

Eh ?   That's it—" I'm not able to pay't,"

Says you.   " You scandalous runnagate !"

Says he ; " you notorious vagabone !

You thief ! aye, murderer !   There's no knowin !

You desperate ruffian," he says, " how dare ye ?

You're a case for pity—are ye ?

Remove him, jailer !" he says, and screws

His mouth like a vice ; but what's the use ?

Jingle the shiners—" Stop ! stop ! stop !

Jailer ! I think we may adop'

A differin coorse.   I think we can,

Jailer," he says, " with this *gentleman.*"

Pay them ! pay the very last fardin !

And, "Raelly, sir!" and "I ask your pardon!"

Justice! Is it justice! Blow them!
Justice! Aw, by gough! I know them—
And should. Why, wasn I took at[1] them there
In Liverpool? And strapt on a bier,
And away at[2] them. And all I done
Was kicked in a window, bein full o' fun
And divilment, and noways drunk, d'ye see;
But just a sup. And fond of a spree
Them times—and *strapped!* (just a taste o' gin!)
Like a dead man goin a buryin—
And in in the dark, and goin a pitchin[3]
On the floor in a sort of divil's kitchen.
And the stink there was there! And the dirty lot—
And never a window, and as hot as hot!
Says I, "I'm respectable connecket."
Says they, "You look uncommon lek it;"
And shuts the door, and turns the key—

[1] By.   [2] With.   [3] Getting thrown.

And them dirty bruteses scratchin away—
You'd think they were in a meadow mowin,
The reglar and complete they were goin!

Well, I never thought much of Harry Cowle
Since that very day; and, upon my sowl,
A man should stick to a friend, he should—
But out of the way the fast he could,
Makin tracks, like a haythen nigger—
The coward! And big! aye, couldn' be bigger!
And strong. And lavin me alone
To tackle the lot! Aw, bone to bone
And flesh to flesh for ever, I say.
Stand by your mates! and fire away!

Why, bless your life! if yandher fool
Had ha' stood, it isn in Liverpool
They'd ha' got the twenty men 'd ha'[1] took us!
But never mind! that's the way the luck is.

[1] Men that would have taken.

And, by gough, it's a comfort all the same—
I made a picther o' two o' them—
And havin no money, the case was clear—
Two months of coorse ! Aw, never fear !

Chut ! Where am I ? Alow or alof' ?
This James, the lad I was tellin you of—
Terrible fond o' the Docthor, you know,
Got out one day, I tell you though,
And bein up to all sorts o' dodgin,
Come unknownced to the Docthor's lodgin,
And tould him Miss Harriet was sent
To a place they calls the " Continent."
So what does the Docthor do but starts
The very nex' day for them foreign parts—
I don't know what country, but middlin far—
About the places they've got the war,
I'm thinkin. But of coorse he was much behind
        her,
And hadn' no track, and couldn' find her.

F

But wandered up and down the land,

Till the money was gone, you'll understand.

And gettin very poor and shabby,

And atin little, and as weak as a babby.

And home at last, and nearly dyin ; .

And James to see him, and bust a cryin—

Aw, bad.   And one of these docthor chaps

That 'd nuss a elephant on their laps,

If he was sick, a reglar limb,

You know, but kind and fond of him—

Well, this young divil took him in hand,

And stuck to him though, and nussed him grand,

Till at last the Docthor was fit for the road.

And that's the time he came to Bigode.

It's a farm that's pretty well up on the mountain ;

And lonely !   Aw, there's no accountin ;

But sick, it's lek, at the heart, and needin

A dale o' peace, like a sort o' feedin,

You know; and glad to be out of Anglan,[1]

For what is there there but wranglin and janglin,

And hurry and scurry, and never allowed

To take your time. And all the crowd,

And—*go it, cripples !*—and the people hard,

And—*out of my road !* and doesn' regard

If you're limpin or laughin ! Aw, very rough,

And savage though ; aye, savage enough—

And uplifted [2] scandalous,[3] and settin their face

Like a flint. Aw, bless ye ! it isn' a place

At all ! I wouldn' give it the name

Of a Christian country. Well, he came

To the Bigode for all, and Bigode is near

Nor'-east from the Lhen, and a step to be there—

About a two mile at any rate—

A little house, but rather nate,

And a terrible prospect of the say,

And mountains stretchin, right away

East and west, and a gill [4] goin slantin

[1] England.   [2] Proud.   [3] Excessively.   [4] Glen.

In front, and a little bit of a plantin;
And situated very purty [1]—
About twenty acre, or from that to thirty;
Middlin land, and a river for sure,[2]
Very nice, and trouts thallure.[3]

Well, it's there the Doctor come to stay,
And nobody knowin, I've heard them say,
Who was he, or what?   Just a gentleman
In hiddlins [4] lek—the way they ran
Common enough them times over there,
And mostly heavy on the beer.
The Bigode's ones [5] was very fond of such—
It's lek—not givin trouble much—
Aw, 'deed, the mistress would ax like a shot
Were they drinkin, or were they not?
And if so be they wasn' drinkin,
" You'll 'scuse me, sir," she'd say, " I'm thinkin

---

[1] Prettily.   [2] Indeed.   [3] Enough.
[4] Hiding, under a cloud.   [5] People.

We'll hardly shuit," she says, says she,

"We'll hardly shuit." Aw, *fond of a spree*

Was the thing for her ; but a dacent woman,

Mind you, and stuck to the house uncommon.

But never axed the Docthor still,

Lookin that down and miser'ble,

And broke to pieces, lek it would be

A fine man fell in ruins, you see—

The way they are. And of coorse *all right,*

Thinks the woman ; and no appetite

To spake of. What ? aw, right enough !

But wondhrin where he had the stuff,

And whenever in the world was he goin to begin—

Wondherin, and wondherin !

And sometimes she'd think he had a way

Of a little stagger at him—eh ?

Or a look of the eye, resemblin drink,

And very promisin, she'd think—

And she'd smile very nice, and pretend to smell
   it—

Aw, bless ye! I've heard my father tell it

(The ould man would laugh!), and sniffin and
    snuffin

As if she felt it reglar puffin

In her face. And, "Aw, Misther Bell! aw, 'deed!

It's the throuble," she'd say, "And no doubt
    you've need

Of a little comfort! Yes—yes—yes!

A little comfort, and a comfort it is—

Aw, general allowed! Aw, well!

Don't regard for *me*, Misther Bell!

Its only too glad I am to see—

And "—a fiddle-de-diddle-de-diddle-de-dee!

And the Docthor, havin a little chaff[1]—

And searched the bed, and searched the laff[2]

To see where was the bottle arrim,[3]

Aye, and every place on the farm,

And the haggart,[4] and pokin every stack,

---

[1] Fun.   [2] Loft.   [3] At him, with him.   [4] Stackyard.

Fancyin she was seein somethin black;

And that curious lek she couldn helf,[1]

Lek playin But-thorrin[2] with herself.

But no signs of drinkin, bless ye! none—

Just wantin to be left alone!

Not but what he was kind, I believe,

Though of coorse he hadn' much to give;

But gave it hearty. Aw, very nice,

And allis had a beautiful vice—

And the flutin, you know; and 'd sit at the door,

And play till you'd hear him at the shore,

Or out on the mountain, he didn' care,

On a big grey stone that was used to be there,

And the very sheep lookin up at him though,

He was blawin through it that strong, you know,

But the pigs, o' coorse, 'd go on with their rootin !

Aw, flootin terrible, terrible flootin !

And all the ould tunes he had them as plain—

[1] Help.
[2] Hide and seek, played round the stacks.

" Kirree fosh niaghty," [1] and " Molly Charane," [1]
And " Hop-tchu-naa," [1] and " Bonny Dhoon "—
Chut ! every tune, every tune !
And that aisy plaised that Misthress Kelly
Was used to say the man was raelly
As good as if he was drinkin hard,
And terrible useful in the yard,
Puttin out dung, you know, and that,
And "no more trouble till an ould Tom Cat,"
She said, " and not noticed in the house;
And mind the childher, or herd the cows,
Or anythin." And never knowin
He was one of the cleverest doctors goin—
Nor nothin about him—better nor wuss—
In hiddlins, you know, in hiddlins jus'. [2]
Aye ! and made some fishin gear,
And agate of the troutses, never fear !
And dozens. And had them for his tay !
And dirty little things any way !

[1] Well-known Manx airs.   [2] Just.

I never could understand the raison

The quality likes them. It's amazin !

But o' coorse ! o' coorse ! And catchin them

Theirselves, you know, and just the same,

But theirselves, and a sort of a newance,[1] you see.

But they're very strange is the quality.

And never much upon the shore

Them times at all, and very wore

And treigh,[2] they were sayin, and fonder of roddin

Till[3] lines, but smilin lek, and noddin,

Whenever he was meetin the men

Gettin water, you know, at the mouth of the glen—

Beautiful water it was—and passin

The time o' day, and maybe as'in[4]

About the boats ; and givin a tune

With the flute ; but goin very soon ;

And the fishermen standin and waitin still,

And wantin to know him terrible !

[1] Novelty.   [2] Sad.   [3] Than.   [4] Asking.

Aw, the casks would be wonderful long a fillin,

And nudgin each other to ax was he willin

To try a cruise; but they didn' dare—

Shy lek—that's the way they are

With strangers, you know ; but hopin for all

The man'd come to, and the slow they'd haul

The painter aboard, and shovin off,

And showin how they could handle their craft—

And terrible curious to know

Was he lookin, and turnin, and keekin,[1] though,

Now and then, and longin—aye !

But not pretendin. Aw, very shy !

For that's the way the fishermen's allis—

Uncommon fond of strangers, and jallis[2]

Of one another, and never the fuss

To make friends afore they'd make friends with

  us—

And likin a man that's big and tall,

---

[1] Peeping. '   Jealous.

And one that's handsome and sorrowful—
And knowin directly like a shot,
Is he a gentleman or not.
Hiddlins! Aye! but aisy to know them,
And likin such, and stickin to them.
But the Docthor wouldn' often stay
To look, but up with the rod and away,
And in on the bushes, and takin the road
Past the Brew, and up to Bigode—
And disappointed, and out to the Head
To see could they get the Pazon instead.
That was the way, I've heard them tell;
But at last they got to know him well—

Aw, well! for behould ye! the cholera came
To the shore, and then it was just the same
Lek it's in the Bible when the Prophet was tould
That time at[1] the Lord to be very bould,
And not to be hidin in yandher place

[1] By.

And booin,[1] like a sort o' disgrace
To a prophet, you know, the lek would be—
But, "Go down and spake to them!" says He—
"Go down and spake to them, you bough!"[2]
And that's the thing he done, by gough!
Aw, 'deed he did—and that's the word
That come to the Doctor. Yes! the Lord—
I do believe it was Him that spoke
That very word, and took and shook
The man in his soul the way he'd say—
"Go down and spake to this cholera!"
And he spoke to it, he did. Aw, the man
Was bould and brave, and he spoke to it grand—
Never was such a Docthor seen!
Never! no never! and couldn' have been.

But the sickness was bad, I've heard them sayin,
And people goin out to the rocks and prayin,
Kneelin in lochans,[3] or anywhere.

[1] Crying.   [2] Poor (creature).   [3] Pools of salt water.

And all the good sucked out of the air.

Aw, bad! very bad! uncommon though—

Black and stinkin!—that's the go—

In an hour, or maybe only a hafe,[1]

And coffined, and tuk and put in your grave

That very night; and turches blazin

Like the luggers shows in the herrin saison—

Only of coorse made slow to burn—

And everybody waitin their turn

Who'd be next. And a man 'd come in

From the grounds[2] very slack, and droppin the chin;

And the foot would be heavy arrim[3] lek,

Gettin out o' the boat—and what to expec'!

And he'd sit a bit on the gunwhale, you know,

And then he'd swallow the heart, and go,

And up to the door, and puttin in his head,

And, *well?* And maybe two of them dead!

And then the cry he'd put out of him!

And prayin and cussin, and shoutin their name!

[1] Half.   [2] Fishing grounds.   [3] At him, his foot.

Yes !   Or never no words at all,

But the dry eye starin against the wall.

And there's some o' them stood out to sea on a tack,

And never no thought at them to turn back,

Nor no heart ; but stupid like in the boat ;

And the tiller with only their oxther[1] to't,

And the head on the hand—and sailin, sailin,

Reggilar, and goin a hailin

At some of these brigs, and hardly the sense

To know, and wakin like out of a trance,

And their eyes all glazed, and, "Look out ! look
    out ! "

And never a word but heavin about,

And in.   And " Is that a way to steer ? "

Says the Whitehaven chaps ;   and cussin them

    there.

And some was givin up everythin,

[1] Arm-pit.

And away to the mountains and wanderin,

And lavin the wife and the childer to die;

And the Pazon after them to try

Could he coax them or shame them; and them
  givin sheet [1]

Like the mischief—and the Pazon, middlin fleet,

And knowin the country well, and 'd nab them

Aisy among the ling, and grab them

By the scruff, and ax them were they men?

And cryin though from glen to glen—

"Come home! come home!"   And, bless ye!
  some

Would swear most fearful, and wouldn' come—

No they wouldn'! but 'd get on a rock

High up above him, and shout and mock,

Blasphemin pitiful. Aw, mad!

Poor things. But others not so bad,

And 'd listen to the Pazon, for all,

And come whenever they heard him call—

[1] Running away.

Aye ! and 'd put their hand in his
Like little childer. Aw, true it is !
And he'd take and lead them very nice
And gentle lek, and the lovin vice,
And the lovin ways that was arrim [1]—you see—
And, "Come, then ! come, then ! come with me ! "
So the men would come, but very wake,
And a kind of silly, the way it'll make
The strongest. Aye ! aw, it might have been
Jesus Himself the poor chaps seen,
And follerin—the way it says
In the Bible. How is this the vess
Is goin ?—I'm not much of a scholar—
Foller, it's sayin, aye ! *they 'll foller*
The shepherd, it's sayin, *the shepherd, though ;*
But a stranger they will not follow—no !
For his voice is strange. So that's the raison—
Aw, the Pazon's vice was sweet amazin,
And he'd have them home ;—aw, never fail !

[1] At him, which he had.

And better and happier a dale.

And some was lookin for 'arbs, and chewin them,

And atin roots, and not rightly knowin them,

And pizenin theirselves. And the ould women that
was doin

Charms and the lek was prayin and booin,

And *hadn' no charms,* and wouldn' let on[1]

They ever had, or the power was gone.

And *Christ to save them! save them! save them!*

And *Go!* But the people wouldn' belave them.

And axin for charms, and some o' them took

An ould wutch, and tore her, and ragged her, and
shook

The very life nearly out of her!

And the women the worst. And *the for! the for*[2]

She wouldn'? And screamin' bad, I'm tould;

And prayin the Lord to save her soul.

And the Pazon come, and "Lave her alone!"

He says, and—*Were their hearts of stone?*

---

[1] Admit.   [2] Asking the reason why.

G

He says, and druv them back. And crawlin
And slobberin at his feet, and callin
For to save her, and grippin his legs like crazy.
And the Pazon terrible onaisy.
And then the lot of them cried out
With a bitther cry, and sent the shout
Right up to heaven, and all the Lhen,
And all the shore, and all the glen
Was just one cry—"Oh, save us, Lord!
Save us according to Thy word!
Save us, oh God of Israel!"

And when the Pazon heard it he fell
On his knees, and he took[1] a shockin[2] prayer—
I've heard plenty tellin that was there—
Took a prayer, I tell ye, for all[3]—
Took a prayer, though, to the full—
A splendid prayer, and all of them aised
Much in their minds, and mortal plaised

[1] Offered up.   [2] Magnificent.   [3] However.

With the Pazon, and the wutch got over her
    fright—
But died, poor thing! I'm tould, that night!

Now, the Docthor heard that cry up there
At Bigode—he did though, and bound to hear,
The sun just settin and him alone
Sittin on the ould grey stone
I tould ye. And the everin very still.
Then the cry come up the hill—
And the other cry was in his heart—
Torectly;[1] and it was—"Start, man! start!"
Aw, he started! he did, for sure—
Aye, that minute! aw, *traa thallure*[2]
Wasn' no word for him—no! no!
Bless ye! didn' the vice say. *Go?*
Aw, I've heard him tellin. And he said he ran
The hardest he could, and took and began
At the very first house, and sent a chap

     [1] Directly.   [2] Time enough.

To Douglas with a horse and trap
For physic and things, and then he stuck to,
And had it out with this cholera though—
Aw, just like David the time he come
And left the sheep with the lad at home,
And a passil ¹ o' little cheeses strappin
On his back for a present to the cap'n;
And then—for all the father tould him—
Yandher brothers must go and scould him.
But it's him that larned them how to fight,
And ups to the giant, and says he, " All right !
Here's at ye ! " he says, " you vagabone ! "
And polished him off with a sling and a stone.
With a sling and a stone—— What's that you're
    sayin ?
I'll trouble ye be so kind as 'splain.
Laughin, too ! What else ? what else ?
The stones the Docthor had would be pills !
Aye, man, aye ? That's very witty—

        ¹ Parcel.

Very !   Raely it's a pity
You're not in the circus, Bobby, too.
They're wantin fools—I dessay you'd do !

Pills !—but come ! no more of this—
It's very improper—that's what it is—
And Scripther, too.   Aw, drop it now !
Listen to me, and I'll tell you the how !
See ! here's the Docthor, and here is David ;
And if you don't understand it, lave it—
The Docthor and David—that's a pair
All as one :[1] now, then, look here—
The Docthor and David—didn' I say ?—
Well, then, here's the cholera
And David—no, that's not it either—
But anyway, two and two together.
David ! David !   Let me see !
How would it be, now ! how would it be ?
The giant—aw, it's aisy to mock—

[1] Just the same.

Swellin out like a turkey-cock,

And gobblin there most terrible ;

And David, with the eye upon him still—

Two and two—and aback of the shield—

And—*I'll give your flesh to the beast of the field*—

Two of a side—I'll have it directly—

The cholera and the giant—azackly !¹

The cholera—that's ould Goliath ;

I got it now—and it's sayin "he defieth

The armies of the livin God"—

The rascal ! And tellin how he was shod,

And the coat and the spear like a weaver's beam—

That's the cholera, just the same—

Aw, I thought I hed it somewhere about ;

But, by gough, it was hard to get it out.

Botherin me, a sling and a stone !

And pills ! I wish you'd lave me alone.

There was another docthor, too, they were havin

¹ Exactly.

Before, that didn' know what he was givin,

Nor why was he givin it—a foolish

Sort of a chap that was comin from Dhoolish,[1]

And couldn do nothin but sit by the bed—

And tap the cane, and shake the head,

And feel the wrist, and count the watch—

An ould man! Chut! he wasn' a match

For Bell at all; for Bell was quick

And supple uncommon, and hearty lek,

And that cheerful that whenever he was by

You couldn' think a man would die—

And that full of life, like makin it go

Into others out of himself, you know,

And just like drivin death afore him—

That's the way. So this ould cockalorum

Saw he wasn' no use at the Lhen,

And cut, and never come back again.

And when the Dhoolish fellow was slantin

That's the very thing the Docthor was wantin,

[1] Douglas.

And had a meetin up at the school,
And the Pazon there ; and Master Coole
That was Captain of the Parish was there ;
And of coorse the captain would be in the chair,
But couldn' put out no talk at all ;
And then the people gave a call
For the Docthor to spake, and so he did,
But the Pazon first.   And the little he said
Was very good.   And *The Lord had sent*
The cholera for them to repent
And call upon His name, and *turn !*
He said ; *and His anger wouldn' burn*
For ever, he said.   And *Our sins was great ;*
But come unto the mercy seat !
He said, *and the crimson would be like the wool !—*
Aw, capital texes !   Beautiful !
So I was tould at them that heard—
And the Docthor didn say a word
Against the Pazon, but bowin, though,
And, "Our respected vicar," you know—

And that. Aw, bless ye! these Englishmen

Can do it with a taste they can—

Chut! of coorse ! and readier far !

The Manx is awkward ! yes, they are !

And excellent advise ! and trustin

They'd never forget ; but for all they mustn'

Lave everythin to the Lord, and sit

With their hands before them; but help a bit

Theirselves. And wouldn the Lord be willin

Of a bit of whitewash goin a spillin

About the place ? And what would they say

To begin and clear the middens away ?

And then an ould fisherman got up

(I believe he had a little sup),

And strooghed the hair, the way with them chaps,

And a little spit and a little cough perhaps—

And says he, " The whitewash 'll do very well—

But middens is middens, Masther Bell ! "

He says. Aw, bless us ! the laugh that was there !

"Middens is middens!" Aw dear, aw dear!

Billy Sayle they were callin him,

But he was never gettin no other name

After that but "Billy the Midden."

And they wouldn clane them; and they didn'!

And of coorse they were right! What nonsense—
    bless ye!

Them docthors, they're fit enough to disthress ye!

Capers![1] What's more comfortable

Till a midden about a house, if you're able

To have a midden, and keep it nice,

And anyways dry? And think of the price

Of dung and potatoes? You can't do without
    them;

And how will you be doin about them

If you havn' a midden! Chut! they're clever,

But hasn' the smallest notion whatever

About dung—not them! And as for the stink—

A midden needn' be a sink!

[1] Folly.

Trim it nice upon the street,

And a midden 'll smell as sweet as sweet,

And very wholesome. I know it depends

Altogether on who attends

To the lek, and careful in the spreddin ;

But of coorse a man 'll be proud of his midden.

Well, the whitewash done a power of good,

And slishin it everywhere they could ;

And the people began to take a heart.

And then some ranters come in a cart

From Foxdale over—a dozen or more—

And had a camp-meetin on the shore,

And shouted there most desperate.

And there was ones come down from the Sandy
  Gate

And jined them, and barrels goin a proppin

Under the tills,[1] and the preachers moppin

Their faces, and all of them at it together,

[1] Shafts of the cart.

And carryin on; and the heat of the weather;
And water sarvin out of a crock,
And singin out like one o'clock,
And roarin till the divils got hoarse,
And the women after them, of coorse!
And some of them was faintin away
Like dead on the shore, I've heard them say.
And "Glory! glory!" was all the cry,
You know the way; and *willin to die!*
And *Come, Lord Jesus! Come! Come! Come!*
And the preacher goin with his fist like a drum
On the front of the cart, and roarin greatly—
Aw, enjoyin hisself completely!
When all of a sudden who should appear
But Docthor Bell! And "What's this here?"
He says; "You rascals!" he says, "be off!
Get out of this!" he says, "you scruff!"
And they said his voice was just like thunder,
And took and kicked the barrels from under,
And down went the cart and the preachers too.

And "Get home," he says, to the women, "do !
Get home !" he says, "isn' that your place?"
He says; "I wonder you've got the face,"
He says, and "bad enough of the others,"
He says, "Aye, bad; but you that's mothers,"
He says, "It's the divil himself that's in't !
Go to your childher!" he says. And they went.

And he turns to the preachers — "Come, make
    tracks ! "
He says. "Indeed! and may I ax,"
Says one of them, "what's the meanin of this?"
And cussin, and squarin up with the fist
At the Docthor; "You're makin very free,"
He says. "Come on ! come on !" says he.
And the Docthor gripped him, though, they said,
Till he rattled the very teeth in his head.
"Let go !" he says, and black in the face;
"Let go !" he says, "let go, if you plaise.
Let go! God's sake!" and chokeder and chokeder.

"Ye dirty herpicrite!"[1] says the Docthor,
And slacked the hoult,[2] "a putty preacher!"
He says, "and cussin like that; I'll teach yer!"
He says, "and wherever do you expec
For to go to?" "I'm one of the elec',"
Says he. "Indeed!" says the Docthor, "indeed!"
He says, "I think I know the breed!
And who's electin ye?" he says.
"You're in the gall of bitterness
And the bond of iniquity," says the chap;
"Come," says the Docthor, "yoke your trap
And cut, and don't come here again!"
"Well, maybe not, though," says the men,
And yokes the cart, and cuts like winkin.

The Docthor was middlin hard, you're thinkin?
Not a bit of him! What sense!
Don't you know what difference
It makes when people is losin heart?

---

[1] Hypocrite.   [2] Hold.

Aw, he was right to make them start!

For, if it's the cholera that's in,[1]

You're wantin all your strength to begin,

And courage to that. Aw, ye better belave,

Or send to the clerk to dig the grave.

Well, one way or another the sickness broke,

And then they were countin who was took—

Just like after a battle, they're sayin,

They're goin about to count the slain.

There was two at Cleator's, and two at Gick's,

And two at Corkhill's—that'd be six—

And three at Kewin's, and Shimmin's four,

Well, now, that'll be seven more;

And six and seven'll be thirteen,

And a baby took at[2] Tommy Cregeen:

And Jemmy Cregeen he lost a son,

And Juan Quayle, and Nelly Bun,

And a boy of Callow's, and three of Creer's—

---

[1] That you have to deal with.   [2] From.

Gels, I think—and at Harry Tear's
There wasn' a soul in the house alive,
So that'll be makin twenty-five.
But that wasn' all. I tell ye, then,
There was forty people dead at the Lhen.
I don't know was I born or not
Them times myself; but that's the lot!
That's the number they were tellin
And no mistake. Ax[1] Neddy Crellin!
All in a month, aye, every man of them!
And never no stone put up to the one of them,
No time, I tell ye, nor money, it's lek.
How could ye expec'? How could ye expec'?

So his work was done, and givin a yawn,
And "That'll do!" he says, and goin,
And all the women wantin to kiss him,
And down on their knees for God to bless him.
And home to Bigode, and not very bright,

[1] Ask.

And took hisself that very night!

Not to say bad, but bad is the best.

And made hisself a sort of nest

In the barn on a loft that was there, and a ladder

And a hatch goin up, and lonesome rather.

And "Nobody," he said, "to come near him

On no account, and never fear him!"

And a bottle of stuff; and "Go now! go!"

And *when he was better he'd let them know.*

So Mrs. Kelly was very willin,

And, faith! she'd rather till a shillin

He'd never come there. Aw, 'deed, she said it,

And of coorse she wouldn' be havin the credit

If he did get better, and "Very hard,"

She said. And *some people didn' regard*

For others, she said. And *it wasn' there*

He took it, she said. *And how was it fair*

To be sneakin home to her, Pazon Gale!

She said, *and the cholera to his tail;*

And her with a family, and the harvis

H

Coming on straight; and nathral narvis
(The Pazon was tellin), *and it wasn' lek;* [1]
And if Kelly had the laste respec',
The laste, she said, *for the wife of his bosom,*
He wouldn' suffer her to nuss him !
No, he wouldn'; but'd up to him straight,
And have him out that very night.
Yes, indeed !   And eyin Kelly,
And him sayin nothin but " Relly ! [2] relly !"
And " Bless me ! bless me !" and hemmin and
    hummin,
And the Pazon tryin to coax the woman,
And done it, too, for anyway
The Docthor got libbity to stay.

But Kellies had a daughter, ye see,
And that was differin totally.
Aw, dear ! you'll easy understan',
A handsome man is a handsome man ;

----

[1] Likely.   [2] Really.

And if so be he's gennal,[1] too,

What 'd you have a gel to do?

For the Docthor would be everywhere,

And meetin him upon the stair,

And houldin herself for him to pass,

And stoopin lek to hide her face,

And him goin puttin his hand on her head,

And strooghin. And whatever he said,

And never thinkin, and just as well.

Aw, it was suction for the gel!

Suction! I tell you. *How do I know?*

Aw, Bobby! Bobby! you're foolish, though—

You're foolish! Is it knowin? What!

Knowin is knowin; mind you that!

Knowin is knowin; and I'll tell ye how

The way's with me. I'll tell ye, now.

There's plenty o' things I never seen,

Nor couldn', and still they must have been;

And when I get thinkin o' them, it'll be drawin

---

[1] Pleasant.

'The head uncommon strong, and showin

The very picthure of them, it will;

And workin and workin terrible.

That's the *knowin.*   And—— Bless me! what's at
  ye?[1]

I wouldn' know anything if I didn' know it that
  way—

Seein it in my head.   That's it!

Chut! I wouldn' give a spit

For a story when it wasn' puttin

Every hair and every button

The way it was, or was bound to be.

Do ye see the thing?   D'ye see? d'ye see?

Maybe not!   All right! all right!

Seein is beein, says Tommy Tight:

And the way the head 'll work is shockin.

Not but ould Anthony's wife was talkin,

And 'd know them well, and livin near—

Anthony's wife!   Aw dear! aw dear!

[1] The matter with ye.

Well, that's the way it was—*like suction,*

Didn' I say? And's been the destruction

Of many a gel, but not of her.

Aw, honour bright! And "Comin, sir!"

And tremblin lek, and quick; and catchin

Her eye away; and watchin, and watchin;

And'd sit in the window, and wait and wait;

And startin when she heard the gate;

And a bit of a ribbon in her breast;

And a sort of a kind of a disthress'd.

But happy and very humble, though!

And innocent. Chut! You know! you know!

Not hopin much. But what's the use!

Lovin, lovin, like the deuce!

Aye! aye! The head is workin? Ler¹ it!

Workin! That's the way you'll ger² it.

But, drop it! drop it! Marianne

They were callin her. And couldn' stan',

And couldn' sit; nor eat nor drink,

¹ Let.　　　² Get.

I tell ye; nor couldn' sleep a wink.

Aw, poor craythur ! That's the way.

And droppin the cups upon the tray,

Sudden lek; and houldin the finger

For the little ones to hush ; and 'd linger

Greatly, and all a kind o' suspicious,

Aye ! lek it'd be a sort of a *vicious*

(The head is workin, Bobby ? What ?)—

And cross with the childher, and sthooin[1] the cat

(Eh, Bobby ? eh ?); and turnin and twissin,

Like a bitch when the pups is goin a missin.

Do ye see her, Bobby ? Run, man ! run !

Hould her ! hould her ! Bobby is done !

Aw, seein is nothin ! Ger along !

Just the strong the head, and drawin strong.

Now, this poor gel was dyin just !

Aw, terrible ! And I wouldn' trust

But it's up on the laft[2] she 'd have taken[3] straight—

[1] Driving away.　　[2] Loft.　　[3] Gone.

Aye, by gough ! the very night

The Docthor come home ; but bashful, no doubt ;

And the mother watchin her in and out,

And got a notion what she had,[1]

And gave it her in style, she did.

And "Lave her alone !" and " Bless my life !"

Says Kelly ; but much afraid of the wife.

And " Stick to your work," says the mother, "you '

    slut !

And let me see you stir a foot

Till them priddhas [2] is peelt." And one by one

The big tears slushin into the can.

(*Workin*, Bobby ?—stronger and stronger ?)

Well, at last the gel couldn' hould any longer ;

For the heart was mostly bust at her.

So aisy ! aisy ! down the stair,

Just about when the day 'd be peepin ;

And hushin the dogs ; and creepin, creepin ;

And slips the boult ; and her head all swimmin,

---

[1] What was the matter with her.   [2] Potatoes.

And her heart in her mouth ! Aw, bless these
    women !
Wasn' she tellin' all the spree
Long after that to Misthress Lee?
And over the street, and never a shoe on ;
And hardly knowin what she was doin—
Aw, a soft sort of thing ! it's aisy belavin—
But the love that was in her, and the cravin—
Aw, soft, no doubt ; and stupid rather ;
And takin mos'ly after the father.
And up to the loft, and stood a bit ;
And never a sound. " He's dead ! that's it !"
She says. " He's dead !" and all the love
Come upon the craythur, and strove
And wrestled with her, till she fell
On her knees beside him. And " Mr. Bell !
I'm here !" she says. " It's me !" she says ;
" It's Marianne, sir, if you plaise ; "
And sobbin lek her heart would brek.
" Don't die ! don't die !" and coaxin lek.

Poor thing ! poor thing ! and what to do ?
Very soft, but lovin, too !

Now, the Docthor wasn' dead, not him ;
But lyin in a sort of a dream—
Deep, though ! deep ! that you couldn' tell
Was there life in his body. So this here gel
Set·to work—aw, I'll engage her !
And kissed his hand like for a wager ;
And kissed and kissed. And a stunnin cure—
Aw uncommon ! Aw 'deed for sure ![1]
Kisses, I mean. *Hands ?* I don't know,
But wantin a dale of patience though.
But he woke at last, with a big long breath
Like swimmin up from the bottom of death ;
And the first he saw was this Marianne,
Which, in coorse, she dropped the hand,
And her own both clapped to her face like a shot.
Aw, clapped enough; and as hot as hot !

[1] Indeed it is.

And trimblin terrible, kneelin there.
Aw, trimblin! trimblin! never fear!
And the Docthor signin for her to go—
Signin still. But she wouldn'—no!
No, she wouldn'!—not a bit of her!—
Wouldn' go, nor wouldn' stir!
And there was the Docthor signin—signin
Most awful!—and her never mindin;
But trimblin still, and couldn' spake,
Couldn' the Docthor, bein that wake;
And signed for her to put her head
Close to his mouth. And so she did.
And whisperin; and "she musn' stay!"
And "for all the sakes to go away!"
And then she got sulky all of a sudden,
And "she wouldn' go then! So she wouldn'—so
    she wouldn',
So she wouldn', *too*," and makin the lip
And sulkin, I tell ye—the little rip!
Then he tried to fie-for-shame her. And then

She bust a cryin. So he couldn pretend

Not to be noticin any more,

And never seen the lek afore ;

And cryin and cryin like the deuce—

And not the smallest bit of use.

So signs for her to stoop down low

(It's like he was workin the eyes, you know,

Havin lost the vice), and " Darlin ! " he said,

Quite hoast,[1] and tryin to sthroogh the head,

But as wake as water, " Darlin pet ! "

Meanin only to coax her a bit,

The way[2] she'd be goin. Goin, indeed !

And the soul at her just beginnin to feed.

Aw, take a baby from the diddy[3]

Just when the mother's gettin it ready !

Aw, bless your soul ! them words was mate.[4]

Darlin ! he said ; *aw, did he say't ?*

And axin him to say it again.

And *was she his darlin ? Aw, was she, then ?*

---

[1] Hoarse.   [2] In order that.   [3] Breast.   [4] Meat.

Of coorse, of coorse! Just think of the drouth
That was in his heart and in his mouth;
And her like butter from the churn,
That fresh, and how could he help but yearn
To the sweet young breath that was comin and
　　goin
Upon his face, like roses blowin
In June, the way it says in the song?
Chut! He couldn'. Right or wrong.
Of coorse! of coorse! So it come at last—
The long, long kiss! Aw, the long it was!
And the rain of tears; and satisfied;
And "Aw, I thought I would have died,"
Says she, and "loved you from the first;"
And he fell asleep with his lips on hers.

Spooney! you're sayin. Aye, man, aye?
Lies! you're thinkin? Aw, divil the lie!
Wasn' it Anthony's wife that was talkin?
Bless your heart! That woman was shockin!

Never a thing that she was tould

But blabbed to every livin soul !

But *Mrs Bell !* *You'd hardly suppose?*

Chut ! Bless ye ! Goodness only knows.

Rather a foolish sort of a craythur !

And women, you know, it's in their nathur,

Colloguin lek, and free of the tongue,

And braggin the days when they were young.

And as for a secret, they cannot hould it.

And, well ! No matter ! The woman tould it.

Tould it ? Aye ! And missin her

In the mornin, and lookin everywhere,

And up on the loft. And *What, what, what !*

And *slut !* and *hussy !* and *Come out of that !*

And *Oh !* *and what would the people say?*

And *Caught with the Docthor in the hay !*

And *Of all the troubles, and she'd had her share !*

And *the Kellies, too !* *Aw, dear ! aw, dear !*

The Kellies ! *The Kellies of Bigode !*

And *Bless her soul !* *she might have know'd !*

And *Oh, the artful!* And *Oh, the sly!*

And the brat to her face, and begun to cry,

And blowin her nose, and about *her character.*

And *What to do?* And *Enough to disthract her!*

And never a word from Marianne;

But the Docthor, which his voice was gone,

I was tellin you, had it nicely back

That time; for kisses is good to slack

The throat, and a little love or so

Will make a man very lively, though—

Very; and so he shamed her grand,

And *How was it she didn' understand?*

And *What was the good to be booin there?*

" You silly woman ! " he said to her;

Aye, "silly," he said; "and this poor child,"

And he laid his hand on her head, and he smiled—

" She knows no evil, Mrs Kelly, mum;

And she thinks no evil," and *Well for some*

If their hearts was as simple and innocent

As Marianne's. And what she meant,

And 'splainin lek, and *For goodness sake!*

Aw, putty talk, and no mistake.

" And this little gel is tellin me

She loves me. Loves me, though," says he.

" Aye, aye ! That's it !" says the woman, then.

" Nice work !" she says. " And 's took to the men

Middlin early, and havn lost

Much time," she says, and *The slut she was!*

And this and that. Aw, the Docthor was mad ;

And " Stop !" he said. And he said, *the bad*

The tongue was at her; and *clane disagusted*

He said he was, *the way she distrusted*

Everybody ; and " Wait a bit !

Wait for all ! God bless me! wait !

I was goin," he says, " to tell the precious

This love is to me ; the way it refreshes

My very soul," he says ; "the way

I clasp it." " Claspin ! claspin, eh ? "

Says she ; "aw, claspin enough, I beliv',

If it's claspin you're at !" And *what would she give*

If she 'd never !—and Kelly a local, too !
And whatever, whatever would she do ?

"Now, listen !" he says; "God bless me ! listen !"
And never saw such a iggrint[1] pessin,
And 'd rather have tould her another day ;
But what could he do, and what could he say ?
Not willin to look like fo'ced,[2] you know—
The way with them chaps that's bringin to—
"What's your intentions ? " that's the shout ;
And had to speak out, and did speak out.
And, "We're goin to be married, this little gel
And me—to be married," says Docthor Bell.
"Goin to be married !—married !" says she ;
And clasps her hands, " Ma chree ; ma chree ![3]
Goin to be married ! And will you have her ?"
Says she. "I wouldn' trust,[4] however,"
Says he. "And will you have him ? " she says

---

[1] Ignorant.   [2] Forced.   [3] My heart.
[4] It seems probable.

To the daughter. "Thank you, if you plaise,"
Says she, and cryin for her life.
"Well, the imperince!" says Kelly's wife;
But jumps for joy, and runs to the laddher,
And down like a shot, to get the father;
And tripped, and groaned a little; but cut
Across the yard with a limp in her foot;
And, "Come, man! come! Make haste, for all!
And bless me! didn' ye hear me call?"
And the two of them up. And "A solemn occasion,"
Says Kelly; and *has his apprerbation.*
And sighin a dale; and *The coorse of events;*
And *A most mysterious Providence.*
And *Maybe a little bit of prayer?*
And *Would they objec'!* And down with him there
On his knees, like a shot; and roared like sin,
And roared till the rafters was ringin again,—
Roared! God bless your soul, the roar!
And blessin their basket and their store,
And the olive branches around their table;

I

And freckenin [1] the hosses in the stable !

Aw, uncommon powerful, I'm tould, at the prayin!

And had him in the house, they were sayin—

Had him in that very night,

And into the big bed with him straight.

So that's the way, you'll understan',

The Docthor married Marianne.

.

And the best of nussin, never fear !

And everybody gettin to hear.

But the woman was right.   Aw, terrible talk :

And " Deed on,[2] Kellies !" and " Yandher gawk ! "

And " Hooked the Docthor ! have she ?   Aye !"

And nudgin, and winkin ; and " Never say die ! "

And " Not a bad dodge !" and " Batin [3] us !"

And all to that ![4]   Aw, scandalous !

For, you see, they will if they gets the chance.

But I'm allis thinkin of the fellow once—

In the Bible, you know—that said to his brother,

[1] Frightening.   [2] Well done !   [3] Beating.   [4] So forth.

"Pull out the mote!"   "Indeed!" says the other;
" Is it motes?" he says; "and talkin to me!
Come out o' that with that beam!" says he.

And how about the lady, then?
Miss Harriet, of coorse, you mean.
Well, that's the thing.   You've got me there!
Aw, got enough!¹   For it's seemin clear,
And promised, you know, and all to that,
The Docthor should have stuck to her.   What?
Stuck to her?   Aye!   Aw, stuck, stuck, stuck!
And there's them that would, whatever the luck,
And no matter for fathers, and no matter for mothers
Some people's stickier till others.

Well, I can't say was he thinkin it betther
To bury his trouble altogether,
And this Marianne like bushes he'd have
Growin there to hide the grave;
Or weak, just weak; or how would it be.

¹ Fairly.

For if she married one of the quality
He might fancy she'd be happier,
Bein used of the lek, and suitin her,
Lek a man, you know, of her own persishin ;[1]
Aye, and the way her father was wishin.
But what for wouldn' she be happy with him ?
Well, raelly, I cannot tell ye, Jem ;
But blood is blood lek, whether or not—
Blood is blood—you'll give in to that.
Aye, blood is blood, says you, *and Bell's*
Was every taste as good as the gel's.
No, no ! my lad ! You're out of it now.
Blood is blood, that I'll allow ;
But there's odds o' blood, man, nevertheless—
Odds, man, odds !—that's the way it is.
Just prick your finger, you're sayin, *and try*
Isn' it the same. To which I rerply,
The same as what ?—as a pig's or a sheep's,
Or Bobby the Bull's, or Barney the Sweep's ?

[1] Position.

All right! all right!   But a common pessin ··

The same as a gentleman's?   No, it isn'!

Aisy! aisy!   Don't cuss, my gillya![1]

I'll have no cussin upon it, I tell ye;

No, I won't!   So there's a stopper!

Let's argufy it nice and proper,

And put it out the way it should.

Now, I'm perfect willin blood is blood,

And chaps like you can't see no furder,

And thinks yourselves——   Oh, murder! murder!

The foolishness a man'll be frothin

When he havn' got knowledge, nor sense, nor nothin!

But we're all from Adam!   So I believe—

Certainly; and likewise Eve!

Fair play for the woman!   The man was the block
   head!

She didn' put the apple in her pocket

Anyway, but gave him share,

And warned afore, but didn' care.

[1] Lad.

Aw, if it's Adam ! that ould scamp !

He's not much of a examp [1]—

The very chap we got all the woe by ;

He's not much of a man to go by !

You're middlin hard up, I do declare,

Eh, Jem, when it's houldin on to Adam you are !

But prick the finger, and then you'll see !

Prick the finger! goodness me !

What for the *finger ?* Look ! here goes !

Let's draw a drop from Jemmy's nose !

Ha, ha ! That'll never do, Jem, will it ?

You havn' got too much, Jem—you don't like to
    spill it ;

Eh, Jem? Were you freckened?—were you freckened,
    lad ?

No, you waren't ! Well, don't be mad ! [2]

Just jokin lek.   I'm fond of Jem ;

But smell that knuckle all the same !

[1] Example.   [2] Angry.

You'll leave it to any docthor—eh?

Now, that's the very thing I was going to say.

A docthor's the man that'll tell ye the brew,

For he'll just be takin a drop o' the two,

And he'll clap his glass, and see in a minute

The little insecs that's swimmin in it.

Insecs ! aye ! *The divil !* you're sayin.

Aisy ! aisy ! Robert Cain !

Divils ! no ! But little roundy things.

Who said *divils ?* Divils has wings.

Well, I think if I didn' know

Nothin about nothin, I'd leave it so.

A cock shouldn' fight if he's got no spurs ;

And them that's had the advantagers,

Lek me, bein thick with docthors that way,

It isn raisonable at ye, eh?

Docthors ! Bless ye ! and who'd there be

Knowin about docthors, if it wasn' me ?

Some right, I think, and seen him strainin

The lek through a sieve, and stuff remainin,

The way with the milk when they're takin and
    silin [1] it.
Aye, and bilin it—actual bilin it !—
Afore he'd be done. But he'd know by the
    smell,
And the colour. Dear me ! It's aisy to tell.
Havn' you never heard them talkin
About blood that was blue (I'll have no mockin)?
Yes, blue ! Well, that's the thing, ye see.
Blue and red ! That's the way it 'd be.
And the smell the same, and natheral,
If you think of the rearin, and feedin, and all.
Only consider the stuff they're gerrin ! [2]
None of your barley-bread, priddhas [3] and herrin,
Or that ; but the best of beef and fowls,
Could and hot ; and salmons and soles ;
And candy sugar and lemonade ;
And cakes, and every pissave [4] that's made ;

---

[1] Passing it through the sile, or strainer.
[2] Getting.   [3] Potatoes.   [4] Preserve.

And puddins and pies, and tarts and jellies,

Takin and slashin them into their bellies,

And wine in buckets! And.—— Chut! It's no
use—

That's the stuff that's workin the juice

Of their blood. And straint[1] and double straint,

Of coorse; and makin it smell like saint![2]

Aw, ye better believe it. But never mind!

Kith is kith, and kind is kind!

Well, for sure,[3] they got married, though;

And the weddin that was at them.[4] Mortal show![5]

Aw, uncommon! Never fear!

And the mostly half of the parish there.

And a terrible speech at Masther Coole,

And ould Kelly himself as drunk as a fool;

But solemn lek; and 'd 'a[6] took a prayer, ᾽

But gripped at the wife, and didn' dare.

---

[1] Strained. [2] Scent. [3] Really. [4] They had.
[5] Very grand. [6] Would have.

And forced to be watched. And the head goin
    cockin ;

And the *hem!* And the knees goin knickin-knockin !

Ready the minute the woman 'd stir,

And her eyin him, and him eyin her.

And—" Oh !" he says, " Thy love possessin !"

And spreadin the hands like a sort of blessin.

Well, that was Kelly—couldn' stan' !

And talk to put him off the plan—

At [1] the Methodists, you know ; but didn'.

And—*Who was yandher that was goin a biddin*

To the marriage feast in Cana there?

And some of them hearty enough, that's clear.

And—*'Scusable to get a little tight*

Just on your daughter's weddin night.

And—*The best of men was apt to be floored*

In a season. And—" Glory to the Lord !"

And—" Dear brother Kelly," and " Yes," and " No,"

And smilin, and " Well to be watchful, though."

And the shuperintendan' goin a bringin

[1] Among.

From Douglas over, and prayin and singin,

The way you know with them Ranthar [1] fellows;

And Kelly sighin like a bellows!

And all made up, though, very nice,

The ould people was tellin. And—*For them to*

rejice,

Says the preacher. And "See the effec' of grace!"

Aw, the Bigode was a shockin comfibil place!

Aw, comfibil—very comfibil!

And handy for the praechers still.

Aw, porridge or puddin, cowld or hot;

Fish or flesh. I know the lot.

Give them a smell—give them a smell!

Aw, bless your soul! It's easy to tell

Praechers is it? Don't I know them?

Bloodhounds isn' nothin to them!

Aw, they couldn' do without Bigode!

Craeture comfits—that's the road!

And—"The labourer worthy of his hire!"

And the little table up to the fire;

[1] Ranter.

And a drop of punch, and shammin weak,
And riftin¹ lek.   And—" Take man—take !
Aw, take ! "   And strooghin down the belly ;
And—" Sesther, sesther !   Relly,² relly ! "
Aw, they knows the spot, and sticks to it,
By gough.   And sure enough it's writ
" Go not about from house to house."
Catch a praecher !   Catch a louse !

Well, the week was hardly flown
Afore there was terrible meetins goin !
Meetins, meetins !   One at the Bull,
And resolutions to the full.
And all the fishermen come swarmin,
And ould Bobby Jinks at them for a chairman.
And another up at the miners' store.
Aw, they said there was never the lek afore.
All the captains about was arrit,³
Captain Row and Captain Garrett.

¹ Belching.   ² Really.   ³ At it.

He was a Cornish man was yandher Row,

Aw, a fuss-rate captain, though.

Fuss-rate enough, and done a speech—

Aw, scandalous ![1]   And Neddy Creech,

That was keepin the store, though, wouldn' be bet,

But up like a shot and seconds it.

And the Pazon had a meetin, too,

And the wardens there.   And what to do.

And Tommy Tite gave a. propogician [2]

For the Pazon to take, and start a petition,

Or whatever they're callin it, and statin

"The general wish."   And then a meetin

Of the whole parish, and givin it out

In the church a' Sunday; and what was it about.

And for all to be sure to come, however.

Aw, 'deed the Pazon done it clever,

And had the meetin in the school,

And people comin down from Barrule,

And everywhere they heard the call,

[1] Splendid.   [2] Proposal.

Fishermen, farmers, miners, and all.

Bless me the jingin and the jammin,

They were tellin; and speeches goin uncommon—

Aw, puttin out fuss-rate, mind you !

At[1] the Pazon there and Neddy Follew,

That was one of the Keys, and Ruchie[2] Quirk,

That was water-bailiff. Aw, dear, the work

That was in ! And the Pazon's petition read,

And *To Dr. Bell, M.D.,* it said,

And *their grateful hearts.* And *the terrible skill,*

It was sayin. And *impossible to tell*

Their feelins lek. And *requestin,* then,

He'd come down from Bigode, and live at the
    Lhen.

Aw, done with a taste, I'm tould. Aw, splendid !

Aw, the man that could, and proper ended—

" Petitioners will ever pray."

You know the way ! you know the way !

And proposed and seconded; and a roar,

[1] By.   [2] Richard.

I was tould, like thunder; and the chaps at the
  door,

Hurra ! hurra ! the way they'd buss; [1]

Hurra ! and carried munanermous—

Munanermous ! Aw, tear your shirt !

Nemine commine—that's your sort !

But they had to build a house for him, too ;

For there wasnt one at the Lhen would do,

Just a corner of a craft [2]

Of Tommy Tite's, that was lettin aff [3]—

Sundered-lek from the rest of the farm

That was there, and a terrible mortgage arrim ; [4]

And the house mortgaged, too. Aw, bless your
  mammee !

Your soul to glory ! That was Tommy !

And Kelly, of Bigode, you see,

Was goin bond and security

For the lot. Aw, well the ould divil knowed

---

[1] As if they would burst.   [2] Croft.   Off.
[4] At him, held by him.

The nice bit o' backin that was in Bigode—

Aye, by gough, and the fishermen
Took a notion to begin
And build a boat for the Docthor; the way
He blackguarded yandher cholera.
Lek grateful-lek; and down at the Bull
Plannin, plannin, to the full—
Aw, plannin regular, but couldn' agree;
And if they could, it's a wondher to me;
For lines is lines, you'll understand,
And allis better to lave it to one;
And did at last, but afore it come
To that, the most of a barrel of rum
Was drunk. Aw, fit enough it's lek
To float her. And Harry Injebreck
Head man agate o' the talkin still,
And arguin, arguin, terrible!
And " Have a builder!" says Harry, " and
    pay'm;"

And " Baem¹ for ever! Give her baem!"

Baem was allis Harry's shout.

And, "God bless me! what are you talkin about!"

Says another; and cussin; and "Baem's your call.

But we'll build the boat ourselves, for all—

Build her ourselves!" and down with the fiss,

And "Hear! hear! hear!" and "Yes! yes! yes!"

And how, and when, and would it be batthar

To have a round starn, or a counter at her;

And carver or clinker, and dandy rig,

Or what, and wait for Shimmin's brig,

Or last year's timber? And "What's your hurry?"

And "Strek while it's hot!" and " Furree!²
    furree!"

You know their way; but left the job

At last to Dicky-Dick-beg-Dick-Bob.

Now, Dicky was a mortal religious chap,

That never drunk nothin stronger till pop.

¹ Beam.   ² Easy.

K

Catch him at Callow's ! Aw, the very pick
Of a fine ould Methodist was Dick—
The rael ould sort; the first that was
When Wesley come preachin on the Cross
In Dhoolish there ; and good men, too !
The pity of them is the few,
And most of them gone to Heaven. Aw, dear !
The ones that's now—— Aw, well, I'll swear
Ould Wesley wouldn' know them a bit.]
" Ger out ! " he'd say : that's it ! that's it !
Aw, worldly ! worldly ! But, Ruchie Fell,
Bless ye ! I remember him well.
I don't think it's ten years since he died—
Ten, would it be, for Hollantide ? [1]
Aye, ten ! Aw, a nice ould man, but streck,[2]
And terrible religious lek.
And *hard to say*, says Molly the Spud,
But there's some o' them is very good.

[1] All Hallows.   [2] Strict.

And that was the way with Dick, for sure—
Aw, good, I tell ye ; good thallure ! [1]

I've heard them sayin that from his youth
The Lord was with him of a truth—
Aw, a sweet ould craythur, whatever there was in
  of him ;
Aw, a sweet ould man, to the very skin of him.
White and dry, you know, and that;
And all the suck and all the fat
Strained out of him ; but as sweet as a bebby ! [2]
And the face, you know, a kind of a slebby [3]
With the shine, and his breath like a sort of a
  balsam,
The poor old thing ! that sweet and wholesome.
But feeble though, and desperate troubled
With these rheumatics. Aw, I've seen him doubled
Many a time ; but patient with such—
Sighin a little, but not so much.

[1] Enough.   [2] Baby.   [3] Slippery.

And a little smile, and a little *hem*—
They're lookin very holy is them.

Well—Ruchie it was, and never dus'[1]
Put a hand but a fit of prayer over it fus'[2]—
Aw, prayin reglar the Lord 'd give signs
To his soul for to help him with yandher lines.
You're lookin! Look then! Look again!
Chut! what's the use for me to explain!
Aye! prayin about yandher lines, d'ye hear!
Prayin the Lord 'd make them clear—
Lek drawin the pecther[3] of them for him—
Lek houldin them there till they're copied arrim[4]—
Lek givin a list[5] to his soul to go
The way the Lord 'd be wantin' you know,
For him to stretch. And rather dim,
And a sort of far off—lek liftin him
To see them lek—the way you'll lif'
A child to see the father's skiff

---

[1] Durst.   [2] First.   [3] Picture.
[4] At him = by him.   [5] Inclination.

Close-hauled for the shore. But what's the use!

Leave it alone, then; and go to the deuce!

I know what I mean. You didn' doubt it?

Well then let's have no more about it.

But it's on my mind, and look here! I don't care

I'll say it, I will, there's a deal in prayer,

A deal! Why, bless your life, I've heard

A chap on a coach that didn' regard

For God or divil, and cocked up as grand

On the dicky there like a gentleman,

And the whole of the coach there listenin to him,

And had it all his own way—blow him!

A skinny chap—I know the crew!

Aw, a reglar cock-a-doodle-do!

"Dear me!" he says, "and aren' you aware

It's all a delusion," he says, "is prayer?"

"It's settled," he says, "at the head men goin,

It's settled!" And an ould man there gave a groan,

And a woman with a child at the breast

Fie-for-shamed him; but all the rest

Was just like sheep; and me rather tight—
Saturday night, you know—Saturday night!
Tom Cowle was drivin himself that Spring—
Teetotal, but reason in every thing,
And a drop is a drop; and civil is civil,
And half asleep! So I says to this divil,
" What's that?" I says. " *Delusion*, is it?
Delusion!" I says. "Look out for your gizzit!"[1]
I says: " here's a little delusion of mine!"
And I took the chap, and I sent him flyin—
What! off the coach? Aye! hove him clear!
I must have broke his neck? Aw, never you fear!
Aw, I wouldn' trust but[2] I gave him a mark—
But I don't know—it was rather dark.
Didn' he follow? Aw, that'll do!
Aisy! Aisy! The same for you![3]

I was talkin about Ruchie Fell,

---

[1] Gizzard.   [2] Rather suspect.
[3] I will extend the same indulgence to you another time.

And the prayer that was at him. Well! well! well!

And prayer is stronger the most that jines—

But prayer it was that done them lines,

And Ruchie's prayer; and never a soul

To back him, but all alone, I'm tould;

All alone—and the first he got

Was the *run;* and, by gough! I know the spot—

The Roman Chapel that was down at the Race,

That's where the Lord was givin him grace

To think the run. And had it as clane,

Aw, bless ye it might have been smoothed with a

    plane

And ready for boultin, the clane he had it—

And the next was the *entrance* [1]—you'll hardly credit,

But I've heard them tellin it for a fac',

He was out two tides on the top of the Stack,[2]

And never a bite; but waitin, waitin,

And the head in the hand, the people was statin,

Till the Lord 'd be pleased, and come at last

[1] Lines in boat-building.   [2] Rock of that name.

In a kind of music, like a sort of a bass,
He was tellin, from the very heart of the sea;
And all the water in the bay
Was playing music; and like as it
The floor of his soul was broke in a rif,[1]
Or a chink, or the lek.   And he took and stooped
Inside of hisself; and a place lek scooped,
And the bearins[2] there lek drew with a pen,
And words, and "For Jesus' sake, Amen,"—
And a light goin sthrooghin;[3] and a A and a O,
Like you'll see in a church.   Aw, he had them,
    though !
He had them, I tell you, as puffec'[4] as puffec'!
And who come by but Masthar McGuffock
(Collecthor McGuffock); and hails him there,
And aboard with him.   And says he, "What cheer ?"
And about the wind; and *how was the signs ?*

---

[1] Rift, cleft.   [2] Lines in boat-building.
[3] Stroking — movement as of lines drawn with phosphorus.
[4] Perfect.

And "Glory!" he says; "I've got the lines!"

Poor thing! like one of them saints in a pecther.[1]

The laugh, they were sayin, tha' was at[2] the Collecthor!

And home to bed.   And the wife couldn' tell

What was the matter with Ruchie Fell.

Stiff as a fit he was, and the eyes

All strained with light, and twice the size.

And "I see her!" he says; "she's afloat! she's
afloat!

God bless the boat! God bless the boat!

The very lines! the very, very!"

He says.   And "Sterry,"[3] he says, "there! sterry!

Wait till Jesus 'll take the tiller!"

He says; and frecknin poor ould Bella

Most terrible.   And "Look! He's gor[4] it!

Crack on!" says Ruchie; "now then for it!

She's true!" he says; "not an inch beyond that!

No she'll not! no she'll not!

---

[1] Picture.   [2] The collector had.   [3] Steady.   [4] Got.

I tould ye!" he says, "the speed! the speed!"
And "Jesus! the Saviour! the Friend in need!"

Aw, the poor ould soul! Ye see the hard
They were workin in him from the Lord—
Them lines. But when she was built, however,
The *Friend in Need* was the name they gave her.
Aye, and couldn' a better fit
Of a name, if you'll only think of it.
A friend in need, as you may say—
The Docthor, you know, and the cholera.

So the boat was built. Aw, they wouldn' be hoult;[1]
And every trennel and every boult
The best of stuff. Aw, clubbed together,
And bound to have it, and didn' considher
The 'spense nor nothin—not a fig!
And three lugs at her—that was the rig—
And raked a bit, three reg'lar scutchers,

[1] Held = restrained.

And carried her canvas like a ducherss.[1]

Aw, the Docthor could handle her like a Briton

But the beauty of that boat was the sittin—

Like a duck! Aw, none of your trimmin sort—

This way, that way; a pig[2] to port;

A pig to starboard; shiftin aft;

Shiftin forward! They're makin me laugh,

Them chaps with their yachts, the onaisy they are!

And the delicate and the particular!

Chut! the trim is in the boat!

Ballast away! but the trim's in the float—

In the very make of her! That's the trimmin!

And, by gough, it's the same with men and women;

For, look here! if a man—— But, bless my soul!

What's the odds! I'm runnin foul

Altogether, and no time to lose;

But "Forge ahead!" says Billy Baroose.

So the Docthor come to live at the Lhen,

---

[1] Duchess.   [2] Pigs of iron for ballast.

Where I tould ye there, just at the end;

Lek in the varginity[1] of the shore;

And the mortal[2] brass plate upon the door,

And "Docthor Bell "—aw, a foot at laste—

Chut! I tell ye, a credit to the place!

And a lot of letters statin what

And who, and a *member* of this and that!

Bless ye! I don't understan'

Their capers! Where's the divil that can?

But the brass plate—— I think I should;

Didn' I stick it all over with mud

One night, and took at[3] the Docthor and hauled

In at him there, and roared and bawled!

But had to take it howsomdever—

My gough! the bitter!—but took it clever.

And out in the street, and cussed tremindjis!

Aw, cussed the very door off the hinges!

Cussed, I tell ye, aw, all I had—

Through the keyhole, you know. Aw, very bad!

[1] Vicinity.　　　　[2] Splendid.　　　　[3] By.

Well, the next thing the boat was goin a presentin;

And then our chaps was rather for slantin,

Bein very bashful for a job like yandher.

And a man they were callin " Nicky the Gander "

Was for havin a tea-party over it,

Bless your sowl! And the whole of the kit

Of the farmers' wives to be givin trays!

And a band from Dhoolish! He couldn' never

take aise,[1]

Couldn' that chap, with his capers—no !

A fuss-rate man for the talkin though !

But I've heard the all he got for his pain

Was " Nicky again ! Nicky again ! "

And laughin, roullin off the settle ;

And " Give Nicky his tea ! " and " Where's the

kettle ? "

Poor little divil ! a weaver he was :

Small—aw, small ; but as bould as brass !

[1] Be quiet.

But it was the Pazon for all that done the deed,
And christened her the *Friend in Need :*
And a bottle of wine, and all correct—
And somethin stronger I'll expect—
And signin her there, like a baby ! And then,
"Hats off ! my lads !" "Amen ! Amen !"
Says the clerk, very sollum. "Hip ! hip ! hip ! hip !
Hoorah !" says the chaps. "Let's give her the
　　dip !"
And "One—two—three," and swings the boat ;
And in the water with her like a shot.
And "Make way for the Docthor !" and a desp'rate
　　crowd,
And the young wife steppin as proud as proud,
And linkin[1] there ; and the chin goin cockin,
And heisin[2] the perricut to show her stockin,
Like any lady ; and a plank, and pretendin
The freckened, you know ; and goin a handin
Over the side at the Pazon ; and a beautiful cushion

[1] Taking his arm.　　　　　[2] Raising.

In the stern-sheets there, and sittin and blushin.

Aw, happy ! I tell ye.   And Harry Corrin

Aboard for a skipper—sailin forrin,

Bless ye !—and sets the lugs, and away !

And sails her up and down the bay.

And ould Kelly, they were sayin, was standin there;

And they could hardly hould him but a bit of
  prayer;

But houldt;[1] and groans, and goes his ways;

And "All is vanity!" he says.

Well childher come to the Docthor though,

Mary, the ouldest—a gel you know;

And then a chap they were callin Will;

And then Miss Katty—that's with him still—

Much younger though, for Will and Mary

Was close together; but the little faery—

A name they had for Miss Katherine—

Was years behind, just lek she'd bin

[1] He *was* held, or prevented.

Run lek off another spool
Altogether; and the yalla hair like gool—
Aw, the Lord's own gool in the very warp of her,
Like strings, lek He'd tuk and made a harp of her
For th' play up.yandher, the way it's sayin
In Revelations—playin, playin,
And the lovely twang goin *pling—pling—pling;*
And "Hallelujah to the King!"
And all the sweet and all the wise
Blowin out in two big eyes
As blue—and the little stalk of a body at her
Lek it's put to a flower to hould it batthar [1]
Up to the sun; but stoops for all,
And hangs the head, and natheral;
For the sun is a bould thing anyway,
Aw, bould enough, and coorse at the play—
But the little body! bless ye! the slandharst [2]
You ever—like these polyanthars—
Convolv'lars—deep in the throat, you know,

[1] Better.   [2] Slenderest.

And the honey guggling down below ;

And the bumbees snugglin there, and pokin

Their nozzles in, and soakin,[1] soakin,

And clartin [2] their legs as sticky as glue ;

And a pleasant sound they're makin too—

And sip and sip—what they call egsthractin—

Bless me ! the pretty them critters is actin ?

But *bumbees—bumbees!* and in and out,

And soakin—— What am I talkin about ?

Little Miss Katty ! Aye ! aye ! aye !

Little Miss Katty. Aw, well I could cry

To think of that little thing—the forsaken

She was at them there, and the way she'd be

    takin [3]

Far over though to the end of the sands ;

And the feet, and the little ankle-bands—

Slip—slip—slippin, or gettin stuck

Altogether in the muck,

And scoopin it out with some shell or another,

[1] Sucking.   [2] Dirtyin   [3] Going.

L

And freckened she'd be took at [1] the mother.

Aw, dear the little lonely thing,—
Just like a bird with a broken wing;
And the lookin up, and the little eye,
Lek axin the for [2] it cannot fly,
And divil the one of the rest 'll stay with it—
The dirty things—that used to play with it.
Fowls is very bad at that;
I don't know about gulls, but lekly not,
That's a dale more innocenter altogether,
Bein strong, and free, and used of the weather.
Poor little thing—the droopin lek,
And the wondrin why! It 'd 'a made ye sick,
The servant was tellin, the way she was knockin [3]
About at them there—aw, boosely [4] shockin !
At the Doctor? No! but the mother ! Aye !
The mother—bless ye ! aw, never say die !

---

[1] Punished by.   [2] The reason why.
[3] Being knocked.   [4] Beastly = abominable.

You were talkin of blood—then what's your shout [1]

To kickin, I wonder! Chut! Ger out!

Kickin, and givin her over the head

With a rowlin-pin—that's what the woman said—

And lookin like it. Bruk [2] complete—

Reglar bruk! And was she gettin mate

I don't raelly know—the little bud!

Aw, the withered—yes! You were talkin of blood!

Well, that's the woman! *Strict!* Not her!

Treacle turned to vinegar—

That's about it! Strict 's no fool;

There's stuff in Strict, that's got a rule

And works it, eh! But yandher woman!

Doeless, doeless, aw, doeless uncommon!

Bless your sowl! it wasn' in her

To *be* strict; and of a manner [3]

The stupidest people 'll be the cruelest.

Reggilar—just doeless, doeless!

And was from the first, I'm tould; but showin

---

[1] What do you say.   [2] Broken.   [3] As a rule.

Some pride in herself, and for her to be goin
For a doctor's wife, and lovin the man,   .
Aw, I dessay lovin, aw, lovin him grand !
Aw, aisy to think ; and buckin [1] up,
Aw, ye better believe it ! the very top
Of the tree was what she was lookin for—
The Bishop, aye, and the Gŏvĕnor,
The Deemsters and the Clerk of the Rowls,
Archdeacons, and that ! Aw, bless your sowls !
The woman was rather short, that's it,
And couldn' put out the talk that was fit
For the lek of them ; nor didn' know
When to stop and when to go,
And chatter—chatter—chatter—chatter,
And all the ladies laughin at her ;
And couldn see the fool she was ;
And the Docthor lookin very cross,
I'm tould ; and wouldn' do at all,
And the higher the flight the worse the fall ;

[1] Sticking, pushing.

And drew the game the soonest he could.

Now, what have you got to say about blood?

Chut! whatever the milk is like the chase[1] is;

So that's your *aequal!* Go to blazes!

But tried, though, hard, and wouldn' give in—

Aw, obstinate astonishin !

And I'm tould when she was puttin a sight on[2]
  Bigode,

She was fit enough to sweep the road,

The grand, aw bless ye ! Feathers flyin,

Like a paycock, all over her; and eyin

The midden, and sniffin, and houldin the scent[3]—

Disagusted, you know, and lek to faint.

And if a pig was killin, though,

Or a sheep—the way with farmers, you know—

Or dung puttin out, or the lek of yandher,

Aw, bless your soul ! it was fit to send her

In 'vulsions, aye ! And "my narves !" she'd say;

[1] Cheese.   [2] Visiting.   [3] Holding her nose.

"My narves!"—and the divil and all to pay.
And the mother and her had words, I belave,
About it there, and *what would she have?*
And "ger[1] out!" And raisonable too,
And wouldn' stand it; and gave her the sthoo[2]
Over the street, and "away with ye, then!"
And might have heard her at the Lhen.

Now, all the Docthor was wantin was only
Fair play for the woman, that 'd been very lonely—
Sundherd from her own people, you see,
And makin no friends with the quality.
Fair play! fair play! and had it plenty;
Fair play! fair play! and hardly twenty—
Aw, had it enough, but wuss and wuss,
Till it's lek the Docthor saw he muss,
And dropt it altogether—straight[3]
Lek you'd do with a dog that wouldn' fight,
Or fightin awkward, and havn' a chance;

---

[1] Get.　　　　[2] Drove her.　　　　[3] Just.

Aw, under your arm with the lek at once,

And pay the stakes, and cut away !   .

You've drew the dog, that's all they can say.

And the divil looks foolish, but he knows what he's at,

He'll eat his supper, I'll bet you that.

Well, the Docthor drew his dog, for all ;

But very cheerful, I've heard them tell,

And kind ; and thinkin how would it be

When she'd have a little family :

Aye, and puttin his heart in it.

But yandher bogh [1] took a sulky fit,

And wouldn' care for nothin, I'm tould ;

And wouldn' laugh, and wouldn' scowl ;

And wouldn' be sorry, and wouldn' be glad ;

And wouldn' be pleased, and wouldn' be mad ;

But just like a log of wood in the house—

Aw, bless ye ! Give me any trouss,[2]

That's got a taste of somethin at [3] her—

[1] That poor (creature).   [2] Slut.   [3] In, about.

I don't regard is it sweet or bitter,
Or what; but these pin-janes [1] of women,
That'll hardly look up when they hear ye comin,
And when ye'll kiss them, 'll put their cheek
Lek a stone, and hardly ever speak,
And never quick, and never slow,
Nor never even a bit of jaw
To freshen a man; but goin, goin;
And what they're thinkin you're never knowin,
But smoothed all over in sulks! Aw, dart! [2]
It's like a slug going creepin over your heart.
Aw, avast with the lek! Aw, give me a fight—
A reg'lar rattler every night!
And make it up; and happy again!
A man can't live upon pin-jane.

And there wasn' a thing the woman hadn'—
Aw, he didn' spare, the Docthor didn',
To plaise her at all,—aw, no, I'll swear!

---

[1] Curds-and-whey.   [2] Drat it.

A most beautiful parlour at her there;

The teens of pounds, I tell ye, the teens;

And mahogany, like any queen's,

And a chandeleer just like an assimbly,[1]

And a lookin-glass against the chimbly,

And the best of chayney; and silks and satins,

And a gool watch, bless ye! and a pair of pattins;

And all complete, I've heard them sayin—

And how the divil could she complain?

And didn'; but you know their way—

And the Docthor workin night and day,

And had enough to earn a livin

Betwix the Lhen and Derbyhaven :

And fo'ced to be away from home

For days; and the far[2] wasn' nothing to him,

But a horse, of coorse, and can't be kep'

On priddha[3]-peelins; and havn' slep'

A week at a time, the Mountain Third[4]

---

[1] That of an assembly or ball-room.   [2] Distance.

[3] Potato.   [4] A division of land.

And Ronnag way; aw, workin hard.

And there's not much jink at the Ronnag chaps,

Nor the fishermen nither, but a goose perhaps,

Or a sheep, or a string of callag or blockin;[1]

Just on the chance, and never knockin,

But in on the back-kitchen, you know,

And down with the lot, and away you go;

No count nor bills, no tally nor check;

But take your change out of yandher lek.

Aw, aisy ways; the most you owed,

A ridge of priddhas, or a load

Of turf, and lave it at the door,

All right! And musn' be hard on the poor.

But had it, aye, and parfact willin,

Aw, value to the very last shillin.

No doubt of that; and swop is swop,

But you can't take a sheep to a draper's shop,

Nor yet a goose. D'ye hear him, Bill?

The lek [2] goin kankin [3] into the till—

---

[1] Fish.   [2] Such a creature.   [3] Kank = note of the goose.

Of coorse, of coorse ! That would be a caper !
" Kank, kank !" says the goose. "Ger out !" says
  the draper.
Aw, dear ! aw, dear! you'd be lookin silly—
" Ger out !" says he. Eh, Billy, Billy ?

But it's aisy obsarved that over yandher,
Sheep or shepherd, goose or gandhar ;
And paid like that, the Docthor couldn'
Have very much over to go for puddin.
But done his best ; and goin still,
And as comfible as comfible !
And no doubt the fish out of yandher boat
Would be lek to be puttin somethin to't.
I tould you the Docthor could manage her splendid ;
But pleasure mostly—the way intended.
Then the childher come, you'll understand !
And takin in a bit of land—
About half an acre—from Tommy Tite.
Aw, it's himself could fix it right—

Cabbages and harbs, ye see,

Convenient for the 'spansary ! [1]

All as nice, with painted rails,

And a limpy gull to work the snails,

And the Docthor delighted; but Misthress Bell—

Well, you know, you couldn' hardly tell;

Just souldjerin [2] up and down the walk,

And the foot like lead and the face like chalk.

Aw, I mind her myself, the long, and the skin

All drew [3] at her, but ouldher then.

But yandher two imps—aw, Lord deliver !

Was the two most desp'rate divils that ever !

Aw, the cheek of the two ! You'll mind them
    Ned ;

And all the tricks and the capers they had ;

And the blackguard talk, and the imperince.

Aw, many a time I've thought of it since,

---

[1] Dispensary.   [2] Lounging (languid, dawdling).
[3] Drawn=stretched tightly.

Where did they get it, for it wasn' cussin

And swearin only till they were bussin![1]

I don't know for the cussin was the gel so bad,

But I believe in spert[2] she was wuss till the lad.

But it wasn' the cussin, for all, so much,

Nor the blackguard talk—bein used of such—

But the imp'rince, and the monkey tricks,

And the mockin, aye; and 'd cut their sticks

Like the mischief, and the innocent face,

If you caught them; but give them the smallest

    'crease,[3]

My gough! the abuse! and then "Three cheers!"

And the stones comin flying about your ears;

And laughin, and away they goes,

And cockin the finger to the nose!

Aw, nath'ral divils, brew or bake,

Aw, natheral; and no mistake!

Natheral; so who's to blame?

But there was terrible little done for them—

---

[1] Bursting.   [2] Spirit.   [3] Increase = start.

Terrible ! for the Docthor couldn',
Bein much from home ; and the misthress wouldn'—
Just starin at them like a cow,
And them carryin on goodness knows how.
And stealin, I tell ye, all over the place,
And darin the woman to her face.

And when they had nothin else to do,
They'd stick to and pinch one another black and
    blue,
And rag and fight, and the crockery flyin
Like dust betwix them ; and the mother eyein
The pair, and "Stop your noise !" she'd say,
And never mindin, and tearin away,
That should have been took across her knee,
And whipped of coorse immadiently.
Aw, I've hommered that little chap, I have,
And the hard and the tough, you wouldn' belave ;
And never give in, but out with the tong,[1]

       [1] Tongue.

And hiss like a serpent, and as strong as strong,

Like iron on the anvil just.

And I tould the mother herself I must;

For the little divil was at me still,

And "If you'll not do it," I says, "I will"—

And bedad I did, and before herself too,

And hommered him well; but, all I could do,

The very next minute he was over the wall,

And cussin as hard as he could bawl;

And sticks and stones and sludge and muck,

Aw, the two of us, I tell ye, had to duck;

And says she, "It's all your fault," she says !

"Why couldn you leave him alone at the fess?"[1]

But the Doctor wasn' knowin half

The bad they were; for they'd plenty of craft

Them two; and the mother wouldn' tell :

And he was terrible fond, was Doctor Bell,

Of the childher, and makin some sort of life

[1] Fir st.

In the house, and a kind of a change from the wife,
That'd sit like a block, and them all springs,
And lookin little innocent things
Enough, but artful, artful still,
And takin advantage terrible.
Aw, well, I've nothing to say agen him,
For the blood of a rael man's heart was in him;
And that's the thing to make others good—
Aw, never spare it! heart's blood, heart's blood!
That's the stuff, I tell ye then,
That'll search the souls of the sons of men;
More preciouser till any pearl,
Or ruby—the very juice of the world,
That keeps its veins from runnin dry,
And tickles its ould ribs with joy,
And sin and sorrow, but never mind!
A power to make us sweet and kind—
In Jesus' heart the stream began,
But it's in the heart of every man;
Isn' it, boys? Am I preachin now?

Aw, well; I'll drop it, but you'll all allow
The Docthor hadn' much chance to order
Them childher aright; so I'll not go furder.
But that wasn' much of a nest, you know,
For a little thing to be born into,
Like yandher[1] I was tellin you of—
The youngest—eh? Not very soft
Nor warm, it's lek; no moss, nor wool—
Bless my heart, the beautiful!
Goolfinches, you know, and the lek of them;
Yellowhommers, too, is much the same.

But aisy! aisy! What am I talkin?
Poor little Kattie. Before she was walkin,
Them two was at her—just like from heaven
A little angel took and given
To them two divils a purpose to treat her
Most boos'ly![2] Aw, the little craythur!
She hadn' no life with them from the fess;[3]

---

[1] That one.   [2] Beastly=abominably.   [3] First.

M

And the mother encouragin them in it—yes !

Encouragin—for, as I'm a sinner,

Aw, there was something woke a spirit in her

At last, I tell ye.   Let be ! let be !

But a spirit of hate and misery—

A spirit that crawled in her soul, and spat—

God save our souls from a spirit like that !

Hard ! it was hard—very hard for some,

But I tell you how the spirit come.

A week or two after Miss Katty was born,

There was a letter, you know, that was evident
    for'n, [1]—

And the Docthor from home ; so opens it,

Bein curious.   And what was there writ,

Do ye think now, in the letter there ?

It was from his ould sweetheart ; aw dear, aw
    dear !

It was though, sure enough ; aw 'deed ! [2]

It was from her, the very screed. [3]

---

[1] Foreign.   [2] Aw, indeed = yes, really.   [3] Handwriting.

And Sir John was dead ; and—*was he the same*

As ever ? and willin to change her name

Torectly ;[1] and off'rin heart and hand—

The talk they have, you'll understand.

And the money, bless ye, and the proppity,

And everythin ; but that wouldn' be

Wrote there of course.   The gel 'd know better—

Aw, a modest, lovin, beautiful letter !

And maybe there's women that 'd 'a seen the thing,

And pitied the two, and took the ring

Off their finger, and said—" I know

All !   Take this ! take this, and go ! "

Not him ! but on with it again,

And swears *for ever and ever, Amen ;*

And clasps her to his heart, Good Lord !

And not another word ! not another word !

But trust, and hope, and confidence—

Some people you see has got the sense.

---

[1] Directly.

So the Docthor came home, and in from the stable,

And the letter a' purpose on the table,

Open, you know (she'd took and read it

To the servant—aye! you'd hardly credit!

Never was a lady, and never would be.

To the servant, I tell ye, as nice as could be:

Aye, and tould her to watch him, too,

To see whatever he would do).

But the Docthor had shut the door, she found;

And listened and listened, but never a sound

For hours; and tried the door at last,

But locked at[1] him, bless ye, and boulted fast.

It'd be daylight when he came out of yandher,[2]
  though,

And up the stairs, but very slow;

And in on the room where the wife was lyin,

And fast asleep, and the baby cryin;

And put the letter on her breast;

And took the child and kissed, and kissed

---

[1] By.   .   [2] There.

The little thing, and hushed it grand;

And put it back to the mother again—

And out and down, and saddled the hoss,

And away with him, like an albatross:

And up to the Mooragh, and seen at [1] a chap

That was cutting turf, and "Stop! man, stop!"

But never a word, but on and on,

And his face was fixed on the risin sun—

The straight you'll see a pigeon flyin,

Lek drew to the art [2] where his love is lyin.

But when the day was rose, he turned,

And the fire that was in his heart had burned

Itself away, and dropped the rein,

And very slow, and home again;

And up to the wife; and just one look

Betwixt the two, and the nither spoke,

And the letter crumpled in the clothes,

And her eye that hard the way a man knows

She knows—the look that leaves no doubt,

---

[1] By.   [2] Point of the compass, place.

The last dead light of love gone out.

So he left her straight;[1] but from that day
He wasn' the same man anyway.
But as for her, she didn' bother
Much about him, bein able to smother
Her soul complete, or maybe for spite—
I don't know, and it's hardly right
To condemn the woman. She done her part
The best she could. God knows the heart—
God knows the heart, but only one thing,
She shouldn' ha' took out of that young thing ;
But did. Aw, did ; and shameful to her,
And wouldn' give her suck no more,
Lek wantin the very milk that was in her
To turn to stone. And thinner and thinner
The little darlin, and cries and cries,
And the dead light in the mother's eyes—
Lek stupid with the heaviness

[1] At once.

Of hate that was swimmin in her breast,

And cloggin her head, and turnin the strain

Of love, till it was bitter again.

Aw, she did hate her though, she did;

And them two imps as glad as glad.

And pettin them, and cockin them up,

And encouragin them; and that young pup—

Aw, it's well he's a head on his shouldhers now,

If so be he has, for I've made a vow

Many a time, and swore it hard,

I'd have his life, and didn' regard

If I'd be hung for the pleasure it'd be

To sarve him out for his villany.

Aw, 'deed it'd 'a¹ been well if he'd been took in
    time,

For the divil had the seed of every crime

And every wickedness deep within him !

Aw, if ever the ould sarpint brewed his venom—

But wait a bit ! You'll hear before long.

¹ It would have.

And a say is a say, and a song is a song.

Now, this foolish mother she stuck to them
Through fair and foul, but special him.
I don't know did she think they were more of
    her own,·
Flesh of her flesh, and bone of her bone,
Because the two of them come to her
When she was what you might call happier;
At laste, you know, lek enjoyin her helf,[1]
And havin her husband to herself:
And little Katty was lek she'd been sent
To mind her of the different.
Lek sayin—"Look! I come the year
The letter come!" Aw, dear—aw, dear!
Whose fault, whose fault is things like these?
Well, I suppose, they're nobody's.
And very likely it wasn' that,
But just lek brewin in a vat

[1] Health.

For years—the stupid and the cruel—
Till somethin 'll stir this divil's gruel,
Lek the letter, you know, from the Docthor's ould
    lover,
And frothin up, and boilin over.
Not much lek the pool that's wrote
In the Bible there, and porches to't—
Bethesda, wasn' it? And an angel comin
Down on a slant, and the water hummin,
And if you could get a chap to put you in,
You were healed directly of anythin.
Aye, but Mrs. Bell, I'll swear, .
There wasn' much Bethesda in her;
But rather like one of these mucky dubs,
Where there's nothin takin[1] but worms and grubs,
Or maybe a leech 'll bite for a change.
Aw, some of these women is very strange !

And now it was, as you may think,

[1] Living.

The Docthor took very hard to the dhrink.

Aw, hard enough! And fell, and fell,

The way I tould you. Poor Docthor Bell!

And agein! You wouldn' believe the agein.

And them two divils, lek their name was legion,

Was wuss till ever,[1] havin nothin to hould them,

And goin to destruction; and I've often told them,

But cockin the head as proud as proud,

And as saucy, and talkin very loud.

And her like a flint. Aw, bould most horrid,

Ye might have struck fire out of her forehead.

And when they grew up the boy was a rael

Unwholsome lookin thing; but the gel—

Aw, 'deed she was handsome, 'deed she was!

Handsome, you know, like a vicious hoss,

And a fire in her eye that was never straight,

But sideways lek, lek goin to bite.

And built to a dot. Aw, a splendid craythur

I tell ye, if it hadn' been for her naythur;

[1] Worse than ever.

That was the divil itself. Aw, the tearin
They had, them too; and the mockin and jeerin,
And every trick. They got a gun
Betwixt them, and what do you think they done?
Climbed up our roof—aw, she could do it nimbly—
And took and fired it down the chimbly.
And the soot comin down in sheets; and the broth
All spoilt; and mother fit to froth
At the mouth with rage, and took a hatchet.
" By gough," says I, " it's now you'll catch it."
But charged[1] so quick as they were able,
And let drive again behind the gable.
" Come here," says mother, " and I'll give you your
    lickins!
Come here," says she, " ye divil's chickens!"
"Good evenin! Mrs. Baynes," says they,
And laughs, and laughs, and cuts away.
And no chance with them; and took in their head
They'd hev some rael shootin, bedad.

---

[1] Loaded again.

And started one of these misty nights
To shoot the turkeys at Tommy Tite's,
That was goin a roostin in the trees.
Aye, they did; and one apiece,
And the other—well, I'll not be denyin,
Sure enough the other was mine.
Coaxin hard. And " Don't be cross !"
And fond enough of a lark as it was,
Let alone a turkey; but chased at a dog,
And had to hide for hours in a bog,
Where the sallies¹ was growin very thick.
And out come Hal, and out come Dick;
And lights goin flittin around the farm,
And the three with a turkey under their arm.
But stuck to them. My gough ! the cheek !
And turkey for supper for a week.
And the lies that was tould over yandher. Well !
And nobody knew but the servant gel,
That was a bit of a divil herself, I belave,

¹ Osiers.

And kept it as secret as the grave.

And once they took up with some gipsies there,

Sthroullers, you know, that come to the feer [1]—

And tents goin fixin on the Head—

A stinkin lot as ever was bred—

Your reglar boosely, thievin tramp—

Till the village took and mobbed the camp,

And wouldn' have them. That's the surt !

And them to take up with such abslit dirt.

Aw, if that wasn' the very high road to ruin !

And nobody noticin what they were doin,

Nor their hours, nor nothin, except me indeed,

That was took for a time to clane and feed

The Doctor's horse, that was bad to keck, [2]

And runnin arrins [3] and jobbin lek—

And mindin [4] me how yandher divil

Come in the stable one night as civil

You wouldn' think what was he schamin there,

[1] Fair.   [2] Kick.   [3] Errands.   [4] Which reminds me.

And me just rubbin down the meer,[1]
And a jenny nettle, and poppin it
Under her tail, and turned and bit
Most savage, just in the thick of the shoulder;
But, before he was a minute ouldher,
I let him have the curry[2] hot
In the ribs, and down with him like a shot.

Took up with the gipsies, didn' I say?
Yes, by gough, and stayed away
The best part of a week, and carryin on
Like the very deuce—aw, the divil's own fun—
Cards and dancin there, and raggin,
And a bottle at him and shoutin and braggin,
And her with her face all painted lek,
And her hair goin flying about her neck,
That she wouldn' be knowed, and actual stopped
The Doctor hisself! Aw, well, that topped
Everything! aw, certain! certain!

[1] Mare.　　　　　[2] Curry-comb.

And axed him would she tell his fortune.

You'd hardly believe ! and a pipe in her cheek—

Aye, staid with them there the best part of a week ;

And me that freckened, for I couldn' tell what

Would ever come of work like that—

Knowin gipsies, and the tricks they have—

Tricks ! aw, bless your soul—you'll get lave ; [1]

Tricks indeed—and went up to try

Could I coax them home ; and fit to cry.

And him as drunk he could hardly stand,

And her with a face as black as tan,

And the eyes the wicked stuff they were brewin,

Like mixin pison with the moon,

That was very clear and full that night.

Aw, it wasn' no use, though I had a fight

With a gipsy chap, and fair play showed—

Aw, there's no mistake ; and took the road

Clane bet, and feelin rather rummy,

Aw, a smart lad that ! and my face in mummy—

[1] You may say what you like.

He could work the fist, that devil, he could;
But another round—but where's the good?

And the Doctor was terrible on the spree
That time; so it's only the mother it'd be,
And her, well—of coorse! and maybe thought
They were at Bigode; but, whether or not,
No notice taken till the neighbours cryin
Shame on such conduct, and was he blind?
And this and that, till at last the father,
Poor man, was forced, you know, to gather
His wits the best way he could, and go
And had them home immadient though.
But that's the time the men gave chase,
And druv them vagabones out of the place.
And not much better, you'll be thinking, bedad,
For a spree like that.   But the talk they had
When they come back, and the gibberish!
Aw, well really I would wish
You'd heard them—another speech, by jingo!

You couldn' understand the half of their lingo—
Not the half!

But poor little Kitty!
Bless me, the divil would have felt some pity
For that little craythur, that was natheral sweet
And good, the child! And the mother'd see 't,
Aye plain enough, but wouldn' regard.
And all the bad things she shouldn' have heard
She had to hear, and trimblin then—
Aw, God is good to such, my men!
And angels puts their wings around
The lek of yandher, I'll be bound;
Aw, there's some sort of music playin in them
That's got a power to defend them
And makin that they're hardly knowin
The sin and wickedness that's goin.
And the biggest rascal you ever knew
I believe 'd been freckened of them two.

N

And Miss Kitty 'd often be coming to me
In the stable, and puttin her head on my knee,
Like a little lamb, and I'd coax her there
The best I could, and sthroogh the hair,
And comfort her lek, and her goin sobbin
And shivrin, and the little heart throbbin
Against my leg. And I'd be tellin her tales
I was makin about little boys and gels—
Just some little bit of a story—
Quite simple—how they were took to glory
Urrov[1] all the trouble; or about the sea,
And the fishes—just comfortin her that way;
And the lovely flowers that was growin down
The deep no line could ever sound;
And the mermaids, and the way they were singin;
And the little bells going ding-a-lingin
On the Flakes.[2] And then she'd lift the head,
And the wondrin baby eyes all spread
Like primroses when the air is sunny,

[1] Out of.   [2] Patches of sand among rocks under water.

And draws them out. Aw, it's then the bonny

She looked, and forgettin all the sorrar.[1]

And then I'd be makin cat's cradles for her,

Or the like of that. And she'd play as nice,

And laugh; and tamin little mice.

Aw, she could do well with the lek o' that,

And terrible watchful of the cat !

Or she'd take my hand, and away she'd trot

To a little meadow the Doctor 'd got

On the river; and the questions she'd ax—

Astonishin ! Aw, fit to perplax

The Pazon; and gathrin yalla lilies,

And these little kittlins[2] that's growin on the sallies,

Like velvet that smooth—Aw, you couldn' tell

The putty,[3] and liftin for me to smell.

And, now and then, of a Sunday, you know,

We'd get lave at[4] the misthris ; and off we'd go

To the Brew, for her to be with Betsy

[1] Sorrow.   [2] Kittens, catkins.   [3] How pretty.   [4] From.

Just for a bit—*our little Petsy*
We were callin her; and sittin beside the river,
Aw, bless ye ! the loveliest thing you ever—
The pecther !¹ Well I've got behind
A tree I have, but never mind—
Just to look, and them not knowin.
And I tell ye the slush of tears 'd be goin
Down my cheek, and laenin my face
Against that tree—Aw, the lovely peace,
And the holy lek, till were we livin
Or dead, and the lot of us in heaven,
It was hard to say—the love, the love !
Oh, the beautiful—Oh, Father above !—
Wrapped in her very heart, and she'd rock
Her to sleep, and smooth the little frock,
And put her down on the nice soft moss—
And then it was my turn, it was—
Mine—Aw, the years ! but every kiss
She'd turn to see was there nothin amiss

¹ Picture.

With the child, and her as fast as fast;

And the shaddhers dapplin on the grass—

And the still, the still; and sweet Sunday light

All siftin through the place, and the light

To my heart; and hope and happiness

In every breath; but God knows best

What *is* the best; and, as it's sayin,

He'll make it plain—he'll make it plain!

Well, at last the mistress took and died

On the sudden; and the Pazon tried

What could he do with the Doctor, for all,[1]

And very willin for him to call—

And talkin and reasonin a dale—

Aw, he was good company was Pazon Gale.

And sober enough, and much respec'

For the Pazon, and humble and quiet lek.

But afore they were done, he'd work it, you know,

Till the Pazon was terrible put to,

[1] However.

And couldn' manage the Doctor, however,

For bless ye, ye see, the man was clever;

Aw, it's clever shockin was the man;

And the Pazon 'd rather for him to go on,

And wonderful talk, and glad to listen—

He said it was *mortal interestin,*

The Pazon said; and that tender-hearted,

And come to convert; but liker converted.

Not the drink! chut! not the drink;

But the Doctor had notions you couldn' think,

And strange, and off the common rather,

And beat the Pazon altogether.

But for all the proud and the clever as well,

He sent that very night for Fell—

Ruchie, you know—the ould man I tould ye;

Aw, he did, sent for him, behould ye!

And prayer at the two, and left him prayin—

Anyway that's what the people was sayin:

And lek enough, for the head 'll be high,

And axin for and axin why;

But the heart 'll be sad, and longin for grace,
Or anythin that 'll give it aise—
Lek you'll see a mountain with the bare bould rock
Goin up to meet the tempest's shock,
And the night is on its head lek a crown ;
And the sky all frost ; but lower down
He's got the kerns,[1] and he's got the firs,
And the veins that 's in his big heart stirs
With the strength of streams, and the soft sweet
    air—
Well, that was like the Doctor's prayer.

I don't know did it last till Monday,
But they got him to church on the mournin Sun-
    day
Very nice, and the childher too ;
And the best of mournin, and all of it new ;
And if ever there was a black snowdrop in,[2]
That's what Miss Katty was favourin [3]—

[1] Mountain ashes.   [2] In existence.   [3] Like.

Nice little things peepin out of the grass—
But the other two was as bould as brass,
And cockin the nose, and tossin the book,
Till the Pazon himself begun to look,
And his vice all trimblin, and his eyes all wet;
And then they tried to behave a bit.

Well, then, the Doctor got terrible bad,
And the life yandher little Katty had,
And growin, you know, for they will, aye, aye !
But very awkward lek, and shy.
And the Doctor says to me one day,
He says (we were fishin out in the bay),
"Tom ! you're a dacent sort of a chap—
Would you mind givin a look if yandher sthrap
Of a sarvint is puttin too much upon
Little Katty," he said; and then he begun—
And the brother and the sister, too ;
And the knockin about and the black and the blue
With the thumpins at them. And would I, then ?

So I said, *Yes, and he might depend.*
Never fear ! So it's a bite he had,
And hauled. And nothing more was said.

So many a time when the tide 'd be flowin
Up to the boat, I'd be takin and goin
In on the back-kitchen at them[1] there,
And never the one of them down the stair
But little Katty ; and at it hard,
And scrubbin and scourin out the yard.
Aw, scrubbin to the very scraper,
And the little knees just wore to paper.
Or down in the cendhars,[2] and the little back
Just broke at her, and as black as black.
And the bellows in bits, and puvvin[3] and puvvin
With the little cheeks. Aw, you couldn' help lovin
The boghee veg.[4] And never a string
Tied in her frock—the little thing—

---

[1] Their back-kitchen.   [2] Cinders.   [3] Puffing.
[4] Poor little thing.

Behind, you know. And the little stays,
And all to that;[1] and the little ways,
And rubbin her eyes, the full of sleep.
And the shamed; and "Dear! I'm like a sweep!"
Aw, the neglected. Aw, scand'lous, though!
Scandalous! And me turnin to
To light the fire; and gettin some sticks
Out of the stable. And her to fix
The tay. And me with a besom sweepin
Fuss-rate. And the trouss[2] of a sarvint creepin
Down, like a cat; and the imprint! Aye!
And the sauce! And laughin fit to die.
And little Katty, turn'd to the shelf,
And pinched but[3] laughin a bit herself,
The foolish I'd look, but maenin well!
Aw, she was a darlin little thing, was Katty Bell.

And the lot of them snorin overhead
Like bulls of Bashan, and their tay in bed!—

[1] So forth.   [2] Slut.   [3] Almost.

Took to them, you know. And 'd roor

That sudden, and hammerin on the floor.

And *Quick—quick—quick!* And catchin up

And flyin. And "Give us yandher cup !"

The dirts ! But when they were satisfied—

Of coorse dependin on the tide,

And no hurry, you know—I'd be takin a smook,

And little Miss Katty 'd be havin a book

And readin to me. Aw, beautiful readin !

Beautiful ! And never needin

To do the big spells. And eyein me

O' one side, now and then, to see

Was I listenin. And that big slut

Hookin herself, and bitendin [1] not—

The sarvint, you know. And the dirty mob

Of a cap that was at her—aw, a reglar slob !

Well, that's the way she got that free

And trustful lek, you know, with me,

[1] Pretending.

That there wasn' no trouble at her whatever
But Tom must know. "Aw, Tom is clever,"
She'd say. And 'deed I was, surprisin—
I was though; and mortal[1] for advisin.

And now I'll tell you the way it was,
And what them divils came to at last.
You see, this Willy Bell was bad
To the very backbone; and the schoolin he had
Done him no good, nor like to do—
Just a quarter, or maybe two,
At the Cullige[2] there; and sthroullin about
All hours, and goin a turnin out
At[3] the masther, that wouldn' have the lek;
And no raison he would, for you couldn' expec'.
That was the schoolin; but nathral sharp
And clever. And only for the warp
Of the divil that was in the very stuff of him,
They'd have made a handy man enough of him.

[1] Wonderful.   [2] College.   [3] By.

But the dirty turn-out;[1] and must try and look
  big,

And up and got the Bigode's ould gig,

And a coult that had hardly a shoe to his foot,

And the Docthor's mare, and to they were put

The way two hosses[2] 'd be goin a yockin

To a cart, and smackin the whip, and cockin

The hat o' one side ; and her with a thing

Like a bugle, and blowin astonishin !

And the pair like brass ; and the fuss-rate it 'd be

To go down to the Cullige, and *let them see !*

And started, I tell ye, from the Lhen,

And into the hedge and out again,

And scorin all the road like a herrin,

Till they come to the Ballabeg ; and gerrin[3]

Locked with the Port-le-Moirey car.

Aw, then the cussin and the war !

And capsizin in the ditch ; and—chat ![4]

[1] Disgraceful expulsion.   [2] Tandem.
[3] Getting.   [4] Chut = tut !

There'd be pounds there—depend on that!

And the little stasha[1] under the nose,

And, my gough! the tasty about the clothes,

And gettin them from Douglas—aye!

Aw, wouldn' be bet. Aw, as high as high!

Just tip-top; and a weskit there

Like these divils of play-acthors you'll see at a
     fair—

All colours, I tell ye! Aw, the chap had notions,

'Deed he had; and the talk, and the motions,

And the ring on the finger—aw, complate!

The buck all over—fuss-rate! fuss-rate!

And often over in Dhoolish;[2] and snakin

About the Barracks, and goin a takin

In at[3] the officers, and lar[4] him

Drink hisself blind, and laughin arrim[5]—

Just for a fool; and not satisfied,

But 'd be more till that—aw, the divil's pride!

[1] Mustachio.   [2] Douglas.   [3] By.
     They let.   [5] At him.

And *who he was, and who he knew,*
And *what he 'd done,* and *what he could do,*
And hintin, and *allis stand by his fren',*
And *the sthrappin gels there was at the Lhen ;*
And intarmined,[1] you know, he'd make them con-
fess
He was wicked enough whatever he was.

So one of them divils come over to see,
Just for a bit o' curosity,
It's lek ; and, for all the capers he had,
I believe the lad was a dacent lad.
But they nailed him—aye ! Aw, they worked him
well—
He was the boy that could do it, was Willy Bell.
And terrible rich, and the money flyin,
And in at the Bull, and all enjoyin
Theirselves though, grand ; and him with the puss[2]
Standin trate for the lot of us.

---

[1] Determined.   [2] Purse.

And Miss Mary soon got agate of him
With her gipsy tricks. Aw, well she could trim
The bait; and I tould ye, didn' I?
The beauty she was; aw, ye couldn'. deny—
But, aw dear, such beauty! where do they gerrit?[1]
Lek it would be an evil sperrit
Had stole a body that was goin a makin [2]
For a pious pessin, and so it'll be takin
All the sweet and all the gud
Urrov [3] things, and soakin them into the blood,
And growin and lookin lovely, but still
It come from hell, and it'll go to hell—
But maybe not—aw, lave it alone!
It's lek the divil knows his own;
And anyway we havin got no call,
For God hisself is workin all.
And there's odds of beauty, and for all the brazen,
You couldn' help it—aw, amazin!
For she 'd keep the eyes upon you, ye know,

[1] Get it.   [2] Being made.   [3] Out of.

And the deep light gatherin there as slow,   ,
Like tricklin into a bowl, till she'd fill it
Full to the brim, and then she'd spill it
Right in your face. Aw, ye'd need to be stones,
For she'd melt the marrow in your bones—
The divil! Aw, many's the time she's made me
Trimble all over—lek she'd flayed me,
With the fire of her look—aye ! aye ! my men,
And me, that hated her like sin !

But this young Captain—well, of coorse !
And the Doctor gettin worse and worse
Them times, and up to Bigode for the hay
Lek he was used ;[1] and the best [of a month
    away—
And terrible talk, and *every wheer !*
And *up the gill,* and *did ye see her ?*
And *bless my soul !* and *bad work !* *What ?*
And *where would it end ?* And this, and that,

[1] As he was accustomed.

And desp'rate work in the Doctor's house,

And carryin on, till this little mouse

Of a Katty was freckened altogether,

And come to me, and not a bad job either—

The boghee veg![1] and the little bress[2]

Like choked—aw, terrible distress

At the child—and *would I come up? aw, do!*

And oh, if I knew! Oh, if I knew!

And *oh, would I come up to-night?*

And—*it isn' right, it isn' right!*

"No, it isn'!" I says. Aw, the red

She got and the shamed,· and the little hands

 spread

Against her face, and turns the quick,

And the sobs goin ruxin[3] up her back!

Think of the shame! aw, the beautiful shame!

Aw, dear! there should be another name

For the lek. When an angel'll be flying past

The gate of hell, you could fancy a blast

---

[1] Poor little thing.   [2] Breast.   [3] Pulsing convulsively.

Of the brimstone — eh ! and him shakin his
feathers—

'Deed they've got to be out in all weathers,

Them angels, aye ! and seein hapes

Of sin. And I wouldn' trust [1] but they scrapes

Their feet middlin careful at the door,

Comin in and steppin on the floor

Very dainty, for not to be silin

The lovely polished gool, and smilin ;

And—*glory, glory to the Lamb !*

Aw, when I think of that the happy I am !

Well, well, let's hope—and the sea all glass—

But the shamed she was ! the shamed she was !

The putty [2] shamed ; aw dear, the sweet,

In a little thing. Aw, I love to see 't.

I was guttin our herrins that time, and I talked

A dale of comfortin things, and calked

The seams of the little bustin heart

The best I could. And *I'd take her part,*

---

[1] I should not wonder.   [2] Prettily.

And " Look here ! " I said, and I showed her my
    knife ;
" Look here ! I'll have that captain's life
This very everin," I said ; " and what's more,
By gough ! it should ha' been done afore "—
Just comfortin lek, the way she'd see
The friend she had. " No, no ! " said she,
And the white as death. " Oh, make him
    promise !
Oh, Mrs. Baynes ! " " Ger out there, Thomas ! "
Says mawther. And *well to keep clear of a quarrel,*
 And rammin the herrins into the barrel,
And sniffin greatly, but looked over her shoulder
At little Katty, and sniffin loudher,
But wouldn' let on [1] for any sake,
But in and got a botter [2] cake,
The thick with sugar, and sthrooghed the head,
And " Go home now ! millish ! [3] Go home ! " she
    said.

[1] Let it be seen.   [2] Butter.   [3] Honey.

And I went with her as far as the gaery;[1]

And then she axed me to speak to Mary.

And the sense she had, and her so small;

And the way she knew nothin, and the way she
knew all!

And—"Is she—is she a wicked gel?"

And—"'Deed, Miss Katty, I cannot tell,"

Says I; "but lookin like it rather."

And *how would it do to tell the father?*

And *no!—aw, no!* And grippin my hand,

And beseechin lek; and *who was her fran'*[2]

But me; and *the good I was, and the nice,*

*And the big and the strong, and the ould and the
wise.*

Aw, dear! "Well, well!" I said; "all right!"

And up to the house that very night;

And not in much notion what to say,

But felt like a fool, though, anyway.

---

[1] Uncultivated field.   [2] Friend.

So I in on the back, and I axed the gel
Was Miss Mary in; and—"Will I do as well?"
Says this trouss, and cockin the cap, and tossin
The head o' one side, and semp'rin, and saucin.
"Hardly," says I.   "Can I see her?" I says;
"I want to spake to her, if you plaise."
"Indeed!" says she; "you're very high!"
And—"Spakin is spakin!" "Go and tell her," says I,
"For all—and look sharp!"   Aw, by gough! she
     went.
You see I was never givin no encouragement
To the lek—no, no!   A dirty thing!
Her to buck[1] up to me, by jing!
Well, she soon came back; and "Go in!" says
     she,
"And I'd rather it'd be you till me."

So I into the parlour; and there she was—
The handsome!   But "all flesh is grass,"

----
[1] Make.

It's sayin. But the beauty and the craft
Of the craythur! and just the tail of a laugh
Left curled on her mouth; and never lifted
Her eyes from the book, nor never shifted;
But aisy to see little Katty had tould them
I was come up o' purpose to scould them.

And—"Good everin," says I, "Miss Bell;"
But rather hesitin. "Aren't ye well?"
Says she. "A cowld, it's lek," she says;
And "ye seem rather shaky;" and *the key of the
chess* [1]
Was away with the Doctor, and the eyes as straight
On the book, but just a slit o' light—
A kink; [2] and the sparklin silver devil
Runnin along it like the bead in a level
You'll see at [3] these masons. "Look out," says I
To myself, "Tom Baynes! Stand by! stand by!
It's comin," says I—"it's fight she manes!

[1] Chest.　　　[2] Peep.　　　[3] With.

Batten down your hatches, Misther Thomas Baynes!"

And I drew a long breath, and I said, "Miss Mary!
I'm sorry now; I'm sorry very"—
And the tight in the throat. "But it's lek it's no
    use,"
I said; and "I must, and I hope you'll 'scuse—
And it's makin' very free," I said;
"But I'm bothered shockin in my head,
And all the talk——" "If I had the keys,"
Says she. "Aw, Miss Mary! if you plaise,
Will you listen to me?" I says—"will you listen?
It isn' my stomach!—no, it isn',"
I says. "No, no!—it's my heart that's in."[1]
"Love!" she says; "oh, that's differin.
How interestin!" she says; and "Come!
Tell me all about it, Tom!
Your heart," she says, "poor Tom!—your heart!"
Then all of a sudden she gave a start,

[1] In question.

And "It isn' me! Oh, Tom! hush, hush!"

And her eyes flew round at me in a rush

Of fire. "Miss Mary! Miss Mary!"—I strove

To get a word, you know. But—"Love!

Love, is it, Tom? And your heart, poor lad,

Is bleedin!—is it, Tom?" she said,

And the sigh! "Oh, God in heaven!" I shouted,

"Miss Mary!" and the red lip pouted,

And the foot went tappin; and—"Well," says she,

"You're a handsome fellow; but Betsy Lee!

Betsy, Tom! Oh, Tom! for shame!"

Aw, her eyes was like the livin flame!

And the smile!—aw, the divil's smile was warpin

Like a leech on her lips. My gough! the sarpin![1]

The sarpin!—and me with the ribs just stove

With houldin my heart, the way it hove

Against them. Aw, I couldn' have stood much
   more;

And if I'd struck her to the floor,—

[1] Serpent.

Struck her dead—struck her dead,—

It'd been better for herself it had,

And a wonder I didn'; but I hoult[1] very strong,

And I said, "Miss Mary, it's very wrong

The way you're actin." I said, "Try, try!

To speak to me like a lady," says I,

"Like a lady," I says, "aw, do! aw, do!

You know what I mean. It is for you,

And for all my heart is sore this night,"

I said. "Aw, dear! the weight! the weight

Of trouble that's fell upon ye all,"

I said, "that's fell, and goin to fall.

Aw, Miss Mary!" I said, "be nice!

Be studdy," I said; "aw, take advice,

And give yandher captain a clout on the head!

He's after no good—not him!" I said;

And *wouldn' she be happier far*

If she was keeping more respectablar?

And wasn' it God that gave her the beauty

---

[1] Held, restrained myself.

And the figgar? And wouldn' it be her duty
To try to be sweet, and pure, and good
The way the Lord was intendin she should?
Aw, try; and all would be for the best,
"And everbody'll love you," I says.

And I kep' the eye upon her still—
The blue on the black! Aw, aisy, Bill!
The cowld on the hot, if you like; and the hand
Went up to the head like a shootin pain—
"Try!" I said, but very low,
Just like whisperin, you know—
Aw, then she was done, and only raison;
And her face in her hands, and her hands like a
    bason
For the full of tears that couldn' help splashin
Through her fingers lek a pessin[1] washin;
And the catch on her breath; aw, it's then the
    Lord

[1] Person.

Was strivin with her very hard.

But I heard a foot goin on the stair,
And I turned very quick, and who should be there
But Willie? We looked at one another
For the best of a minute; aw, studdy, rather,
Studdy; but he couldn' hold on,
And the eye fell slant. And then he begun
And *who the this, and who the that !*
And *what in the world was she snivlin at ?*
And "What have you been talkin about,
Tom Baynes?" he says. And "Just get out!"
He says, "get out of here!" he says.
My gough, the tinglin in my fist!
"Now, I'll be plain with you, Willy Bell,"
I says, "I'll be plain; you know right well
What was I talkin about, for you were standin
The whole of the time upon the landin.
Now, then," I says, "you're a gentleman,
And I'm—— However, that's your plan—

Listenin, is it? You snake![1] And you heard
All that was sayin—aye, every word !"
Aw, he turned his back, and he goes to the sisther,
And says he, "look up," and he took and kissed
   her.
"Judas !" I shouted, "Judas ! traitor !
Devil !" I said, "let go the craythur !
The Lord is with her." "Oh, no doubt,"
Says he, "but we know what we're about."
And I looked, and she just give one long shiver,
And the face was as hard and as wicked as ever.
"Help, help ! my God," I cried, "help now !
She's lost ! she's lost !" "Come ! blast this row !"
Says he. Aw, I made a step, and I put
My face into his, and fut to fut,
And "Devil ! Devil ! Double die
Of a devil ! I can see it in your eye !
I know it ! I know it !" "What ?" he said.
"What, indeed ! What, indeed !

[1] Sneak.

Will I kill ye now?" I says.   Aw, he shook

Very bad.   And I took and stuck

My fist in his handkecher, and I gave

Just one good twiss.   "Come, lave then! lave

Lave go!" he says, and the teeth goin chatterin

"By gough," I says, "you're a beautiful patterin [1]

Of a gentleman."   And her as quite [2]

All the time; but the soft, good light

Of God was gone out of her, and starin

Lek a kind of stupid, the way its appearin

With people that's drunk that sleepy stuff—

Laudanum, is it?   Lek enough:

But didn' offer to help him at all,

And the divil pinned against the wall;

And puffin and cussin what would he do.

"Come out!" says I.   "No, I won't, for you!"

Says he.   "You coward," I says, and I ground

My knuckles in his windpipe, and down

He went like a sack of potatoes though!

[1] Pattern.   [2] Quiet.

"You're a murderer!" she said. "No, no!"

Says I; "there's twice too much life in him yet."

Aw, you might as well ha' talked to a idiot

As to her, the way she was then. So I went,

For I was intarmint[1] to be off immadient

To the Bigode to see was the Docthor in trim

To be fit to come down and spake to them.

And afore I got to the end of the street

I heard the click of a horse's feet,

And a Douglas car. And "Wuss and wuss!"

Thinks I. "And now it's who'll be fuss!"[2]

And I ran like the mischief. And there he was

The poor old Docthor, and a staemin glass,

And the one tum[3] over the other, twiddlin,

You know. And middlin sober—middlin.

And—*For all the sakes to come at once,*

Or lek enough we'd lose the chance—

And the work that was in.[4] And "Docthor, come!"

[1] Determined.   [2] First.   [3] Thumb.   [4] There was.

"Stop," he says, "till I finish this rum;"

And suckin it sweet, aw, the last grain of shugger.[1]

And then this stupid ould hugger-mugger

Of a Kelly, the grandfather, you know,

What would hould but he must go?

And huntin for his stick, and wrappin

His stupid ould neck. And—*What might happen,*

And—*The Lord over all.* And—*Wouldn' it be well*

To begin with prayer? "Eh, Docthor Bell?"

"No," I said, "Mr. Kelly," I says,

"There isn' no time for this foolishness."

"You scandalous rapprerbate," says he,

"For shame!" he says. And down on the knee,

And by gough he gave tongue that all the glen

Might have heard him. "All right! Amen, Amen!"

Says I. And glad they warn'[2] in liquor,

But half out of my senses they wouldn' come quicker.

And the hummin and hemmin; and *the death of*
    cowld,

[1] Sugar.   [2] Were not.

And " Be careful, Kelly !" and " Bless my soul ! "

And, " What's become of yandher stick ? "

Aw, enough to make you sick.

But off at last ; and slow, though, very,

And groanin and prayin like ould Harry !

And " Yes, Docthor Bell," and " No, Docthor Bell,"

And " It's lek it's better to go, Docthor Bell? "

And " Are ye there ? " and " Wait now, wait ! "

And " It's very coorse," [1] and " I'm all in a heat ";

And me like disthracted.   And, *was I suttin ?* [2]

And stoppin and strugglin with a button—

And " D—— it ! Mr. Kelly," I says,

" It's too bad altogether, it is."

" O," he says, " young man, I see !

I'll have a little talk with you," says he.

" What is it sayin," he says, " in John ? "

" Good Lord ! Mr. Kelly ! come on ! come on !

Come on ! " I says ; so he come ; but sighin

Very bad, and lek to plyin [3]

[1] Rough (weather).   [2] Certain.   [3] Repeating.

A text to hisself. And got them down
To the Lhen at last; and people round
The door o' the Bull, and 'cited rather,
And nudgin when they saw the father;
And over to the house, and there—
Of coorse! of coorse! Aw, never fear!
Gone though! and no use to be frettin;
And Pazon Gale in the parlour sittin
As patient; but thinkin very deep,
And little Katty fast asleep
Before the fire, or *was* a fire,
But this beautiful servant was off to enjoy her
Talk with the neighbours; and just a rakin
Of dust in the bars. Aw dear, the forsaken!
The miserable! the miserable!
And the Pazon with his elber on the table—
The Pazon, aye; for when the child
Seen their actin, she run like wild
Up to the Church, that nothin couldn' stop her;
And *was she too little to reach the rapper,*

Or couldn' work it, the Pazon was sayin,
She put her face to the window pane,
The Pazon said, *like a little ghose,*[1]
He said ; and the flat of her little nose
Just like a peep-show, he said it was,
Don't you know? a bit of glass
And flowers goin squeezin under it ;
Eh? and a little mossel[2] of spit,
And *give me a pin*
To stick in my chin—[3]
What? of coorse ! of coorse ! you know—

Aw, the Pazon was funny though.
Well, he took the little sowl in his hand,
And away the two of them went to the Lhen
The quickest they could, but it was all up then.
But still the Pazon thought he'd stay
A while on the chance. So that's the way,
Her on the mat, and him on the chair,

---

[1] Ghost.   [2] Morsel.   [3] Words used in a childish game.

The time the Docthor and Kelly got there—
And me? Aw, yes, I went in with them;
And the first thing ould Kelly give a hem
And "Peace be to this house!" he says,
And somethin chapter, somethin vess,[1]
And behoulds the Pazon, and "Oh," says he,
"Oh, what a opportunity
For a little improvement," he says, *aw dear!*
And would we objec'? Just a little prayer?
Or how would a taste of exhortin' do?
And "Pazon Gale, I'll lave it to you"—
And "This young man," he says, and cockin
His eye on me, ".is given to mockin—
Yes!" but the Pazon didn' regard him;
Lek enough he never heard him,
But. he had a hould o' the Docthor's hand,
And if ever a man looked into a man
With love and power it was him that minute:
Aw, the very shiver of love was in it—

[1] Verse.

The long long love, the healin love,

The Comforter, the Heavenly Dove;

Aw, the white without a stain,

Lek you'll hear the praechers—"Return," they're

sayin,

"Return, thou Holy Dove, return,

Sweet messenger of rest ;

I hate the sin that made thee mourn

And druv thee from my breast."

And then little Katty woke from her sleep,

And she looked around and she gave a leap

At the father; and hung, and hung, and hung—

"You'll 'scuse her," says Kelly, "she's very young"—

But the Pazon said—"Mr. Kelly," says he,

"We'd better be goin"—and turned to me—

"Come, Tom," he says, just whisperin lek—

And out with the two of us as quick

"That's the salve he says that ll heal

His wounds." "I purtess,[1] then, Pazon Gale!"

Says Kelly, very sharp, "I purtess!

It was a opportunity, and it shouldn' ha' been
　missed."

But the Pazon coaxed him very nice,

And they went, and I could hear the sweet ould
　vice

Like music hummin through the night,

And I strained to hear for the joy and delight,

And strained till I couldn' hear no more,

And urrov[2] the glen, and took for the shore,

And in; but my heart was very sore.

And only off with my shoes and jacket,

For I was intarmined[3] to see would they be at the
　packet.

And gave the ould woman slip fuss-rate,

And never touched a mossel o' mate,

And got to Douglas middlin arly.

[1] Protest.　　　[2] Out of.　　　[3] Determined.

Aw, by gough! but they bet me farly,[1]

For where must they be off to all the while

But Ramsey, and sailed with the Mona's Isle?

The Mona's Isle!—I wish she'd ha' sunk!

I was just that mad that I went and got drunk,

And I couldn' tell ye when I got home—

But I saw yandher driver, and I gave it to 'm—

As innocent there upon the Cross![2]

Aw, I had to do it, the mad I was.

So that was Misther Willy Bell

That sould his sisther. Still!—keep still!

Sould her! Didn' I see the notes?

Didn' me and Tommy Oates

See him crispin them in his fingers

At Callow's? Didn' we, by jingers?

And didn' I tell him *he had his wages,*

And he'd burn for it, through all the ages

Of hell, I said, and the dirty sniggle

On his face—aye, just like a worm 'll wriggle

[1] Fairly.   [2] Market-place.

Under your calker;[1] and didn' we take them
Urrov[2] his hand, and didn' we cake them
Together, by gough! and soak the whole o' them
In a pint-jough[3] there, and make him swallow
   them?
Aye, did we! and a goodish few
Made it up to kill him, too,
And tould he wasn' safe at the Lhen;
And cut, and never come back again.
No, no!—by gough! he's not such a fool,
And he's for a bully now in Liverpool.

And did this Mary ever come back?
Yes, she did. She tried that tack,
Maybe about a two years after;
But of coorse this fellow had took and left her
Long afore that. She came about
Of a summer's everin; and the Docthor out,
And Katty with him, and the new sarvint they had

---

[1] Heel-tip.   [2] Out of.   [3] Ale-mug.

Come runnin down the shore, and she said
The *free she was, and the condescandin,*
And the lovely drest, and there was no depandin
To the talk with people. " Aisy, Bess ! "
Says an ould fisherman there. "We know what she
   is ;
And, by gough ! " he says, "she'll pack her traps
This very night ! " and calls the chaps,
And gets a cart, and away with them though,
And me a follerin rather slow,
And thinkin a dale ; for, for all the sinner
She was, the door shouldn' be shut agin her ;
It shouldn', I tell ye—it shouldn' be,
If she's anyways took in her conscience, ye see—
Aw, no !—and done with her wickedness,
And longin, longin, longin for rest.
" God help the lek ! " thinks I ; and the cart
Goin rattlin on. " Will I take her part ? "
Says I to myself. " Well, well ! I'll wait ; "
And the cart goin stoppin at the gate,

And "Come urrov[1] that !" says Bobby Brew ;

"Come urrov that !" says all the crew ;

"Come urrov that !—come urrov that, will ye ?"

And says Bobby, "We're not goin to kill ye ;

But we know very well how your bread is arnin[2]—

So you'll off by the packet to-morrow mornin.

Now, come !" says Bobby—"come, and make
  haste !"

So she come—she come! My God ! the face !

Just a graven image cut out of stone—

The tight and the glazed; you'd hardly ha' known

Was it a livin woman you'd got,

Or some figgerhead for the divil's yacht !

And goin a heisin at[3] them there,

Straight[4] like a coffin upon a bier,

And a cross-board at them, and a wisp o' straw ;·

God bless ye ! the lek you never saw !

---

[1] Out of.   [2] Earned.
[3] Being lifted by.   [4] Just.

And givin in, and noways vi'lent,

And because she was silent, they were all of them
  silent;

Aw, you might ha' heard a pin—

For all the world like a buryin.

But the pitiful! the pitiful!

And along the street, and past the Bull;

And, "Aw!" I said—"aw, give her a chance!

Aw, just this once!—aw, just this once!

And wait for the Docthor! aw, do! aw, do!

Aw, Masther Brew!—aw, Masther Brew!

Can't there be no mercy?" I said;

But ould Bauvy[1] only shook his head,

And over the shore; and then the women

Come out, and one by the name o' Shimmin

Up with a clew of goss[2] to strek[3] her,

And others tryin to draw the kecker;[4]

But some was shoutin, "Where are ye goin?"

---

[1] Bobby.   [2] Bunch of gorse.
[3] Strike.   [4] Kicker, for tilting a cart.

And— "Aw, the poor thing !" and "Lave her
    alone !"
And just when we come agin [1] the well,
Who was there but ould Ruchie Fell?

And—"Come, then, Ruchie ! give her a prayer !"
And the innocent ould soul that was there
Stuck to at once, and prayed away
Till we got to the other side of the bay,
And keepin up, and peggin along
By the side of the cart, and prayin strong,
And the two hands clasped before him like this ;
And at last he took and gave out a vess [2]
Of the "Buryin Psalm," and middlin right,
But then they hushed him for th' [3] be quite,
And tould him he hadn' got the tune,
And left him standin in the moon.

But Mary Bell ! oh, Mary Bell !

[1] Over against.   [2] Verse.   [3] To.

What she was thin'kin, who can tell?

Sittin there as firm and straight

As a crowbar; and all the lovely light

Shinin off her like a block—

Lek you'll see it shinin off a rock.

If it wasn' the sittin, you couldn' have tould

Was she dead or alive. And—"Is there a sowl

At her,[1] is there?—or a body just?"

Thinks I to myself. Aw, *dust to dust.*

Bless ye! we might ha' been agate of a biler

On the Foxdale road[2]—when, ·behold ye! ould

    Smiler,

The Pazon's horse, and the Pazon's trap,

And the Pazon himself! And—"Stop, men! stop!"

We were about the Ballayonna, you know,

·When we met him, Ned, and turnin slow

On the bridge that's there. "What's at ye[3] at all?"

---

[1] Has she a soul?

[2] Carrying a steam boiler up to the Foxdale mines.

[3] What have you?

Says the Pazon, backin agin the wall;

And—"Hullo!" he says, "Thomas! is that you?

Aw, dear!" he says, "and Robert Brew!"

And *what were we afther?* and *we gave him a start,*

And *who was that we had in the cart?*

So they tould him; and the Pazon tried

Hard, but they wouldn' be satisfied.

"Let her see her father!" he says;

And *the wrong,* he said, *and the wickedness*

They were doin, he said, *it was awful! awful!*

"And more till that—it isn' lawful."

"We'll chance the law," says the fellows then;

But, by gough! the Pazon was at them again.

And *who were they to judge the why* [1]

The gel come home? lek [2] *enough to die,*

Says the Pazon. Says Brew, "She's not the surt!

And I tell you, Pazon, we'll have no such dirt

At the Lhen," says Brew; "so there now—there!"

[1] Reason why.   [2] Likely.

Aw, he was the chap to spake. " You were allis
    severe
And hard, Robert Brew! But listen to me !
I've nussed this child upon my knee;
I've christened her in the church," he says ;
" And now—and now—she's come to this !"
And, " Oh, our Father in heaven !" says he,
" Look down on her in her misery ;
And melt, oh, melt! these hearts of stone !"
And, " Havn' you childher of your own ? "
He says to the chaps. And there wasn' a word
For a minute maybe, and all that was heard
Was the river, cryin down the gill,
And houldin their breaths—aw, very still.

Then says the Pazon, " Mary Bell,
Have you come home to be a good gel?
In God's name, Mary ! in God's name !
Is that, is that the for[1] ye came !

[1] The reason why.

Answer !" he said ; but she wouldn' spake
Then says Bauvy, "I know the sake[1]
She come well enough : it was for the little sister—
Little Katty—to try could she get and 'list her
In the same sort of work." "That's it ! that's it !"
Says the others ; "little Katty—to get
Little Katty !" they says. "Little Katty—aye !"
And, "Stick to it, Bauvy !—that's the why !"
And *Miss Katty was the darlin of the shore,*
And she'd been knocked about enough before—
And they wouldn' have it, they said, *and 'd rather*
See her in her grave ! and *the father*
Was a very nice man, but he wasn' able
To take care o' the child ; and gettin feeble,
They said, *with the drink, and far too soft ;*
And it was Katty—Katty they were thinkin of—
Little Katty ! Aw, then the head
Come down at last. "I'll go !" she said—
Yes, but sulky-lek, you know ;
"Drive on the cart !—I'll go ! I'll go !"

[1] Reason why.

Then the Pazon gave a terrible sigh,
And he says, "The Lord is always nigh!
I'll go with her myself, I will!"
And out of the gig, and on to the till,[1]
And into the cart. And, "Thomas, good lad!
Take care of the gig!" And—*the bad!—the bad!*
And a mortal trimblin in his vice,
And sittin beside her as nice as nice.
So on we druv, with the cart in front,
And the gig behind, and just a grunt
Now and then at[2] Bauvy; but me that beat
I was nearly fallin off the seat—
And the Pazon talkin very low,
But what he was talkin we'll never know;
But it's lek[3] *to repent,* and *the aisy yoke*—
The way they're talkin, and right to talk—
Pazons—yes!
    So that's the way
We got her down on Douglas Quay;

  [1] Shaft.   [2] From.   [3] Likely.

        Q

And we waited till the packet started;
And the hobblers[1] there was terr'ble divarted
With the Pazon! And, *What a stunnin old limb!*
They were sayin; *and a gel with him!*
Aw, these Douglas hobblers is shockin rough,
Though there's some of them dacent chaps enough,
But free o' the tongue, aw, 'deed they are,
And ready for any sort of war.
But the Pazon didn' mind them, no he didn',
Just like an ould angel, the way he was spreadin
The peace around him, lek shook from wings
Round and round and round in rings—
The holy, the holy, and the true!
Aw, the beautiful and the lovely too!
Aw, bless him! bless him! He'll wear the crown,
Will Pazon Gale! And up and down,
Up and down on yandher pier,
And that stubborn thing that was at[2] him there,
Whatever he could do or say—

[1] Boatmen.　　　　　　[2] With.

But she broke with the breakin of the day—
Broke when the day broke! Well, raelly now
Them's the only words—I don't know how—
Was it the Prince of Darkness was put to flight,
For he couldn' stand the sting of the light;
Or was the red that ript the East
Like a finger pointin to the place
Where she had to go? Or did God look out
From the pillar of fire, lek when he was about [1]
Yandher Pharaoh, and all his host
That come tearin there along the coast,
And braggin that Moses couldn' help but laugh,
Chariots! had they? and the wheels comin off!
Aye, but, however, she sobbed a dale,
But what she said to Pazon Gale
Was never known; but you could see like a shot
The Pazon was aisier after that
For her to go. I can't tell if she hadn
A godly sorra—for tears 'll be sheddin

[1] Engaged with.

Very bad, and even prayin,
But a godly sorra, the Bible is sayin —
Of course, and—*lek never to do it again*—
Do ye see the thing? We'll drop it then.

And so she was put aboard at last,
And ould Bauvy says—"Will I make her fast
To anything?" But the Pazon went
To ould Captain Craine, bein well acquent,
And—*would he give an eye to this young pessin?*
And—*the 'spectable*, and *very distressin*—
"All right!" says the Captain, but middlin gruff,
"All right!" "And is it goin to be rough?"
"No!" he says; and "Now for the shore!"
And turns his back. I belave he knew her.

Well, that's all I've got about Mary.
And home with the Pazon, and terrible weary
The two of us till the Pazon heard
A lark that was singin very high,

And all like quiverin with the joy—
Then said the Pazon—"You'd hardly belave
There was sin in the world, to hear that stave—
Sing on, my bird! sing on!" he says,
"Your song of love and happiness!
Sing on, brave bird!" and the ould head dips,
And I seen the prayer on his lips—
Aye—but didn' spake again
At all. And so we come to the Lhen.

Now, I don't know azackly[1] the years it would be,
But it was once I was home for a while, you see,
With the ould woman, bein in two minds
Would I stick altogether to the lines,
And give up the sea; and I'd had my sup
Of troubles, you know, but mortal took up
With little Simmy, that was growin grand—
Eh, Simmy! Are ye asleep, my man?
Look at him! rolled up like a ball!

[1] Exactly.

Ha! pretendin! Aisy all!

Well, I think it was a everin[1] in May,

Or June, a yacht come into the bay,

A terrible beauty, schooner rig,

Fore and aft, you know; and big

Tremenjus—two hundred register

At laste, I'm thinkin; and they anchored her

Inside of the Carrick. And a boat come in,

And a sarvint, and orders at him to send

A Docthor aboard, if so be there was one

At the Village, and then for him to go on

To Douglas, and get them Docthors too—

Idikkilis![2] as if Bell wouldn' do!

But that's the way! and a gig at the Bull,

And yoked in a crack,[3] aw, a gig to the full—

Aw, it's Callow's could do it, and off like a shot,

And then, ye see, Docthor Bell was got;

And the boat that come had to stay behind

For stores, and so he went in mine.

[1] Evening.   [2] Ridiculous.   [3] Horse put to immediately.

The sun was settin when we fetched,

And there was a lady lyin stretched

On a bed on the deck, for she wouldn' stay

Below as long as it was day.

So that's the raison they satisfied her.

And the son and the husband standin beside her,

And the awnin furled, and the last bit of light

Shinin full on her face—Aw, the white! the white!

And "Here's the Docthor!" and makin room,

And the young man leaned his head on the boom;

But the old man took the Docthor's hand,

And led him to her, you understand—

But when she seen him she gave a cry,

And, "Oh, you're come to see me die!

Oh, Edward! oh—perhaps it's as well—

Oh, Edward Bell! Oh, Edward Bell!"

And he fell on his knees, and he bowed his head,

"Harriet! Harriet!" he said;

But the Lady Harriet was dead.

Yes! it was her. You *knew it was comin?*

Aw, the very woman! the very woman!

For when the Docthor wrote to her

To say he was married, she didn' care

For nothin at all, but only to go

Somewhere out of the way, you know—

Lek a craythur that's goin a runnin[1] over

'll creep in the hedge to try and recover—

Aye, but a taste of pride with it all,

Aw, pride no doubt! and natheral!

For what had she done but axed a man

Would he marry her, and the fella ran—

Well, not azackly that, but still—

Aw, she was feelin it terrible.

And went and took a little house

In the counthry, and just a couple of cows

And a little land, and a lady's maid

She was used of lek, that could make her bed

And that, and this man they were callin James,

---

[1] That gets run over.

You'll mind, that was tellin me all the games.

Wasn' it him that came ashore

In the boat to send the Docthor to her?

And off without a bite or a sup

'To get the Douglas Docthors up.

Wasn' he tellin me over ·our tay—

We'd been whitin fishing in the bay

That ev'rin—aw, a dacent chap,

And the fond of the whitins he couldn' stop—

One after another—and *aw, the delaycious !*

And him and me was very gracious.

Well, she come to live in this little place,

But she couldn' get a mossel of peace;

For of coorse the rich she was and the beauty,

There was hundreds comin to pay their duty,

Lek makin application, lek sportin

Their figgers afore her. I doubt it's coortin

It'd get[1] with us, but the quality

[1] It would be called.

Must have a differin name, ye see.
So I believe at last she was fairly fo'ced
To take a husband. And like a ghost,   ·
They said, the day she was married. Aye !
But a rael good man, and tervil high ;
And a splandid scholar, you'll be sure,
And kind, and givin a dale to the poor;
And wise and careful all the same—
Lord Brockley they were callin him.
And she never had no child but the one—
A boy, you know, and reared at them grand ;
But the mother took very much to failin,
So the docthors thought a little sailin
Would do her good. So every year
They were havin a trip in the Vivandeer,
They were callin her. And sixteen hands
All tould, and sparin no expense.
Aw, a splandid vessel, splandid, though !
And that fitted up, you'd hardly know
Were you standin in a ship or a shop.

And stewards there—aw, just tip-top ;

And the paintin and the gool—you never !

And the lookin glasses ; but, however—

So it seems this time they'd been over to Dublin,

And rather rough, and the sickness troublin

The lady bad.   And bound to shake her

Roundin the Calf.   And waeker and waeker,

Till at last they got freckened, and had to give in,

And come to an anchor at the Lhen.

So that's the way, the very fit.[1]

And wasn' it nice now ?   Wasn' it ?

And her ould sweetheart, and all !   Just so !

Aw, beautiful !   Aw, lovely, though !

And the wonderful for him to be nigh,

Lek it'd be a pleasure for her to die.

Yes, yes ! you're right !   Aw, 'deed, for sure ![2]

The woman was dyin happy thallure.[3]

And coffined there at Masther Cowle—

Rosewood—rosewood !   Bless your soul !

---

[1] Exactly.   [2] Most certainly.   [3] Enough.

Satin linin, satin trimmin,

Just like a pianna, I heard some women.

And put aboard the Douglas boat,

And Masther Cowle himself attendin to 't.

And the proudest day of his life, I'll bet.

Aw, poor Lady Harriet !

Now afore she was married she tould the Lord

About the Doctor, every word.

And hard to do it's lek it'd be,

But " Bless ye !   What's the odds ? " says he.

Aw, thrumps the both, and 'd out and spake ;

Aw, the rael breed, and no mistake.

So this Lord Brockley seen at once

What was up, and capital friends—

Capital !   Chut !   The man had sense.

There was a sayin of his the people had

When the two was ither side[1] of the dead.

Then says this Brocolo—" Poor dove !

---

[1] One on each side.

I had her truth, and you had her love."

But the young chap never knew nothin at all

Till now, and it sunk in his heart like a ball

In the teak. And the pecther in him he'd drew

Of his mother—ever since he knew—

Shivered, And had to put it together

The best he could ; but differin rather,

Aw, differin. And the very next day

He took to the mountain straight away.

I don't know did he think some angel would stand

On the cairn with the pecther in his hand

For him to copy ; but there's no accountin—

There's queer things seein on the mountain—

Aw, queer enough. And the air, you know,

That keen ; and no accountin though.

But I know a bird that 'll whistle ye down

From any mountain, I'll be bound,

A little bird. A hen or a cock ? ·

No matter. " Come down from yandher rock !

Come down !" it's sayin.   And, by gum,

When that chap pipes, you'll have to come.

Aye, will ye.   Aw, it's thrue, it's thrue!

Do I mean little Katty?   Of coorse I do.

Little?   No!   But a woman grown,

And a joy for your heart to think upon.

For whenever she was gettin fair play,

With them two divils goin away,

She took a body, and she took a chin,

And a figger there astonishin.

And very careful of the father,

Aw, terrible, that was difficult rather;

Bein studdier, but apt to get dry,

And slippin into Callow's on the sly.

But she had a way to keep him in

Of a night.   And grog, but 'lowancin.[1]

Did she water it?   No!   God bless my sowl!

Do ye think she'd ever be that bould

To water the father's grog?   Aw, dear !

---

[1] Putting him on allowance.

Water? No! Did ye ever hear?

No, but 'd play with him, and coax

To get the bottle from him. And little jokes.

And he'd reach out his hand, all shaky lek,

And she'd put her arms around his neck,

And kiss him, and laugh, and look in his face;

And all the little lovin ways—

And the hand goin fumblin. And then, I'll be
   blowed,

If she wouldn' be shovin a pipe in the road,

And grips and sucks, and it lighted at[1] her

In a crack. And " No matter," he'd say, "no
   matter !"

Aw, the grand ould man. And a bit of a smile,

And knew what she was up to all the while.

Havn' I seen them? And the proud she was

When she got him to bed with only a glass !

But, bless ye ! that was years before ;

[1] By.

For the Docthor come urrov[1] it more and more,

Like urrov a drame, like urrov a fog.

And the man could sit and take his grog

Like a Christian. Moderate lek, that way—

Moderate—that's the time o' day,

Just with the glory he was takin

In the daughter, and the happy she was makin

The heart of the man, and the beautiful

She kep' the house, And never dull,

But as bright as bright. And then, for all,[2]

He began to see the lusty and tall,

And the handsome she'd got, and the full in the
    hips,

And the sweet talk runnin off her lips

Like water off an oar on the feather;

And the sensible; and altogether

The woman she was, and knowin a dale.

So, by gough, he spoke to Pazon Gale,

And the two of them stuck to like fun,

[1] Out of,   [2] However.

And taught her everythin under the sun—
Taechin ! Bless ye ! reggilar !
Aw, they loved to be taechin her.

And books and copies, and sayin and writin,
And the ould pianna—aw, just delightin—
That was it, delightin you know—
And the terrible fast she was larnin though,
And all about doctorin and bones,
And a hommer at her choppin the stones,
That they're sayin is rather suspicious o' meltin,[1]
And showin the lines the world is built on.

So you see the gel was just in her bloom ;
And no chance but Misther Harry Combe
Would be seein that—just a puffec[2] flower,
Lek the sun 'll be shinin after a shower,
Puffec, you know, in every part—
Aw, the little spot was in his heart

---

[1] Show symptoms of having been melted.   [2] Perfect.

Afore he left the Island—yes!

Chut! Bless your sowl! he couldn' miss—

But didn' say a word, but back

The very next month! Aw, he wouldn˙ be slack,

Wouldn' yandher lad! Aw, very keen,

And as handsome a chap as ever was seen—

Aye, Harry Combe they were callin him,

And still it wasn' the father's name—

Curious! And lookin bad,

Not havin the name your father had—

Lek somethin wrong, you know, but wasn';

And there's plenty of them 'll have a dozen.

But I don't know. But, however, it come,

And not long about it, the way[1] with some;

But out and spoke, and axed her straight

Would she be after marryin him. "All right!"

Said Katty, at least—you understand—

Well, of coorse—aw, a very nice young man.

And it's lek there'd be a dale of blushin goin,

. [1] As it is.

And *what did he mane?* And *hardly knowin;*
And all to that;[1] but come at last,
The little word that makes all fast—
The little word—and whenever he gorrit[2]
He'd put a kiss upon her forrit[3]
Like on a queen—at least I'm tould—
The quality!—But bless your sowl!
And it was beautiful to see
Their little ways—aw, love-ely.
'Deed I've been hidin in the goss
A' purpose to see how happy she was,
The darlin! And hardly right, you know,
But still for all—just so, just so!
Of coorse, and the world is full of slandher;
But angels might have looked at .yandher.

One everin I seen them on the How—
Christmas Head they're callin it now—
Yes, yes! you're right; that's the name they hef,[4]

---

[1] So forth.   [2] Got it.   [3] Forehead.   [4] Have.

And the one taken and the other left—
The Bible is sayin—but lower down
Just under the cairn where the Rose was found,
And an ould well there the people was thinkin
Very holy, and goin a drinkin
For cures, or maybe laevin a pin
Or a halfpenny for luck to be in,[1]
But rather lek them Romans, eh?
With their 'dolatry; but hard to say—
Sittin there beside the well,
Aw, a pleasant spot and peaceable,
And these penny-walls[2] and little ferins[3]
Has got a very putty appearance;
And the water that's in tremenjus cowl[4]—
So I was takin a little sthrowl,
Bein under orders to jine a ship
The very next day, and a longish trip,
And you never know, and—aye, man, aye!
Lek it would be a sort of good-bye—

[1] To be = for luck.   [2] Wall pennywort.   Ferns.   [4] Cold.

So of coorse pretendin not to know them,
But blest if they didn' call me to them,
And then they tould me the way it was,
And *goin to be married for Michaelmas.*

And "Tom," she says, "you've been a brother
To me," she says, and a kind of a smother
In her throat, you know, lek she couldn' refrain,
And the tears come rushin like the rain,
And she caught my two hands with the two of hers,
And she looked the long look in my face
And "I'm so happy, Tom," she said,—
"Thank God," says I, and I bent my head,
And she pressed her hands against my lips,
And I kissed the little finger tips.
"Thank God!" I said, but I couldn' say more—
And I went, but when I got down on the shore
Thinks I, "This 'll never do at all—
Booin away like a funeral—
And, by gough, I don't like to see her cry,

And, by gough, I'll put her in heart," says I.
So I turned, and stood, and I gave them a cheer—
I did though—terrible sharp and clear—
"Hoorah! Hoorah!" and up with the cap
Agin the wind, and down with a flap
In the water; but seen her laughin there,
Laughin, laughin—never fear!

God bless her—she's a married woman
Now, and a little family comin;
And livin in England, and got the father
Very nice though living with her.

So that's THE DOCTOR. And now, my men,
I think it's time to be turnin in.
Good night! It's feelin to be rough.
You liked little Katty? Well, that's enough.